"Why are you trying so hard to get me to leave?"

"Because I can't stand the thought of anything happening to you," he replied through gritted teeth. Normally, Lawson was so careful in how he carried himself, but right now, Sarah could see the restraint cracking—she could see him giving in to this feeling between them.

"You're being selfish," she shot back. "You just want me gone so you don't have to deal with whatever this could be between us."

"That's not it at all," he replied, moving closer to her, hands coming to her arms, like he was holding her in place. Making sure she wouldn't slip through his fingers. Her breath caught in her throat, and her eyes flicked down to his mouth and the stubble across his strong jaw. Her fingers itched to reach out and touch it, to feel it beneath her fingertips.

"Then tell me to stay," she breathed. "Show me that you don't want me to go."

PROTECTIVE WARRIOR

JANIE CROUCH

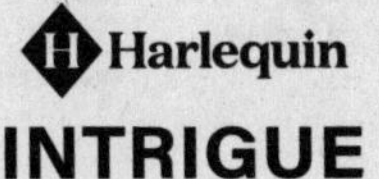

To Harlequin. Thank you for giving me my start and for seeing me through over twenty-five books.

Recycling programs for this product may not exist in your area.

ISBN-13: 978-1-335-18905-9

Protective Warrior

For questions and comments about the quality of this book, please contact us at CustomerService@Harlequin.com.

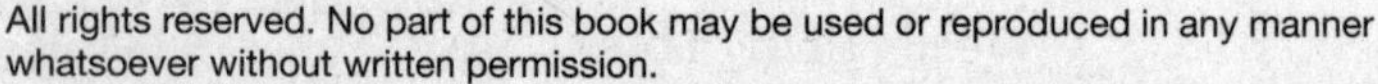

Harlequin Enterprises ULC
22 Adelaide St. West, 41st Floor
Toronto, Ontario M5H 4E3, Canada
www.Harlequin.com

HarperCollins Publishers
Macken House, 39/40 Mayor Street Upper,
Dublin 1, D01 C9W8, Ireland
www.HarperCollins.com

Printed in Lithuania

1 2 3 4 5 6 7 8 9 10 LIT 28 27 26 25

Janie Crouch writes passionate romantic suspense for readers who still believe in heroes. After a lifetime on the East Coast—and a six-year stint in Germany—this *USA TODAY* bestselling author has settled into her dream home in the Front Range of the Colorado Rockies. She loves engaging in all sorts of adventures (triathlons! two-hundred-mile relay races! mountain treks!), traveling and surviving life with four kids. You can find out more about her at janiecrouch.com.

Books by Janie Crouch

Harlequin Intrigue

Warrior Peak Sanctuary

Protective Assignment
Protective Lawman
Protective Refuge
Protective Warrior

San Antonio Security

Texas Bodyguard: Luke
Texas Bodyguard: Brax
Texas Bodyguard: Weston
Texas Bodyguard: Chance

The Risk Series: A Bree and Tanner Thriller

Calculated Risk
Security Risk
Constant Risk
Risk Everything

Omega Sector: Under Siege

Daddy Defender
Protector's Instinct
Cease Fire

Visit the Author Profile page at Harlequin.com.

CAST OF CHARACTERS

Lawson Davies—Former CIA agent and co-owner of Warrior Peak Sanctuary. Runs the tactical unit.

Sarah Peterson—Resident psychologist at Warrior Peak Sanctuary.

Xavier Michaels—Runs the day-to-day operations of Warrior Peak Sanctuary.

Hannah Davies—Lawson's little sister and longtime employee at Warrior Peak Sanctuary. Engaged to Xavier.

Cade Thatcher—Former soldier who now works at Warrior Peak Sanctuary and helps with tactical missions there. Engaged to River.

River Robertson—Works at Warrior Peak Sanctuary as an assistant to the counselor. Engaged to Cade.

Aaron Ward—Former cop at Kings Mountain PD and was Bailey's training officer; now handyman at the lodge. Engaged to Bailey.

Bailey Masters—Former cop at Kings Mountain PD; now cop in Blue Ridge. Engaged to Aaron.

Chapter One

“Those are only going to last for a few days you know,” Lawson Davies pointed out to his sister, Hannah, as he leaned against the wooden doorframe of the lodge’s entrance, watching as she fiddled with her most recent flower bed additions. “What’s the point of spending so much time pruning them?”

“Because I enjoy it!” she protested, shaking her head at him as if she could hardly believe how obstinate he was. “Just because the flowers aren’t going to last long doesn’t mean there’s no point in doing it at all.”

He cocked an eyebrow. “You’ve been obsessed with those flowers all year.”

She paused her pruning, rounding on him with the shears. “Yeah, so I’m going to enjoy them when they’re actually in bloom,” she pointed out, jabbing the shears toward him demonstratively.

He held up his hands in surrender. “Hey now, show mercy. It was just an observation,” he protested.

She laughed. “If you keep bad-mouthing my flower beds, you’re going to get it,” she warned him. “What are you even doing out here, anyway? Did you just come by to annoy me?”

“Keeping an eye on you,” he replied. “I don’t trust you with those shears. I’ve seen how clumsy you are.”

"When I was a kid! You really think I'm as bad as that now?"

"Yeah, I do," he retorted.

She let out an irritated snort. "Well, guess you better keep your distance, then," she warned him playfully, holding up her shears. "I might trip and stab you with these."

"And you'd still care more about your flowers," he teased her.

"You're damn right I would!" she replied. "I've worked hard. I want to enjoy the fruits of my labor."

He grinned as she turned her attention back to the blooming flowers running alongside the path that led from the main building to the residential cabins in the woods beyond. He really didn't mind that much that his sister was so intent on spending her time making the flowers look perfect. After everything that had happened in the last couple of years at Warrior Peak, he couldn't blame her for hanging on to something she had total control over.

God knew, he'd been doing the same thing. Working on the lodge had been a relief these last several months. It helped ground him from all the recent troubles they'd endured here, and the fact that he was one of the people who got to call the shots was just a bonus.

He was all about structure and order and balance, which went back to his military and CIA days. And seeing all the employees working hard on the rebuilding, and all the improvements they'd done, made all of the hard work worth it.

Warrior Peak Sanctuary had been a safe haven and dream come true for Lawson and his best friend and business partner, Xavier Michaels. It had become something they could really be proud of. Over the years they'd helped military and law enforcement, and, more recently, domestic-abuse survivors find themselves and their strength again. To be able to rest and recuperate from injuries and refresh their bodies, minds and souls in a peaceful, safe environment did wonders for a person's overall being. They had also been able to bring in more professionals and add a variety of different activities to aid in the healing process. They'd seen large improvements with all the new additions they'd made available to their guests.

Since the last attack on the lodge, they'd decided to do an overhaul on certain aspects of Warrior Peak. The main one being the addition of a small separate building next to the main lodge for Sarah Peterson, the lodge psychologist, to have her new office. They'd also added a small cabin next to it and turned that space into new living quarters for her. The section in the lodge that had been her office before had been renovated and turned into additional rooms for guests.

He hadn't been as sold on having the two spaces next to each other, but after Sarah had rattled off the list of benefits it provided her with them being side by side, who was he to argue? She loved it, and that was what mattered.

Seeing that the residents enjoyed the space separation was a good thing, too. They seemed to feel a little more comfortable being able to go to a separate space and not feel like they were being watched and judged when they went to their therapy appointments. It lifted a small weight off their shoulders and that was important. Lawson wanted them to feel safe and secure in their sessions and everything they did for their recovery.

Lawson had also noticed that Sarah had seemed a bit more hesitant to use the makeshift office they'd originally done up for her in another part of the building while they were constructing the new space. It was farther away from the main entrance and all the hustle and bustle of activity in the lodge. He had his suspicions that she felt isolated being farther away from everyone, and closed off from getting fast help, should she need it. Lawson hoped that would not ever be the case again.

He knew she had been struggling since Jed's attack on her previous office. He'd terrorized her and torn her safe space apart in front of her eyes in a fit of rage. A large man ranting at a petite, sweet, fragile woman like Sarah… It set Lawson's blood boiling every time he thought about it. He'd do whatever he could to make sure she felt safe at the lodge again, to help get her back to the happier, more carefree and confident woman she used to be.

The plunge tub had also been a good addition. It added a bit of excitement to the place. It had many therapeutic benefits—that was why Lawson had suggested adding it in the first place—but it had turned into more of a challenge for those staying there. It had become a test for people to see how long they could last in it and then rush back inside to warm up.

Those who did manage to use the tub for its benefits seemed to enjoy it, though. Lawson had even tried it himself a few times, but he wasn't sure he entirely saw the benefits of freezing your ass off for the sake of your mental health. Damn, at least it woke you up in the morning, better than a coffee ever could. That had to count for something, right?

And even though he loved picking on his sister, he had to admit, the flowers she'd been working so hard on around the lodge looked nice. The bright blooms popped against the soft green of the grass, especially in the sunlight that streamed through the trees beyond. Times like this, he could see why the lodge worked as well as it did. Why it was a place where people were able to actually leave behind the horrors of what they had endured before, and relax in the peace of this environment.

A peace that was suddenly shattered. The door to Sarah's new office slammed open and raised voices sounded inside. Suddenly, Toby Miller, one of her new clients, came storming down the path, his eyes blazing with anger.

"Hey." Lawson stepped out onto the path with his hands held open at his sides. "What's going on?" He looked worriedly between the angry man and the open door.

"She's freaking crazy," Toby snapped, jabbing his finger back toward the office.

Lawson followed his gesture, and saw Sarah standing in the doorway, her face pale, blue-green eyes wide, her shoulders tensed up toward her ears. She looked stiff enough to crack in half.

Lawson sighed. "Go inside," he told Toby. "Cool off for a minute. I'll talk to her, alright?"

"Fine, but I don't know how I'm supposed to accomplish anything with her acting the way she is," he growled as he stomped down the path and back into the lodge. Lawson turned his attention back to the therapy office, where Sarah had already ducked back inside.

"You want me to check on her?" Hannah asked, eyes wide and hands clenched into fists at her sides.

Lawson shook his head. "No, it's fine, I'll handle it," he assured her. He had been feeling particularly protective of Sarah lately, after everything that had happened with Jed a few months ago. He imagined that she was seriously spooked by the encounter she'd just had with Toby because of it. He squeezed Hannah's shoulder lightly as he walked by her down the path.

He reached the door of the therapy office and noticed it wasn't completely closed. He pushed it open and stepped inside, glancing around. Sarah was slumped on to the small couch opposite her desk, her shoulders still drawn up toward her ears, and her whole body trembling.

"Hey," Lawson murmured to her softly.

She jumped, her head snapping around like she was suddenly looking for danger to strike. When she saw who it was, she let out a long sigh of relief.

"Oh, Lawson, it's you," she replied, pushing a hand through her ponytail, and patting her blond hair back into place. "I—I'm sorry, I don't..."

"It's okay," he assured her. "I sent Toby back to the lodge. He's going to be fine when he cools down. Are you alright?"

She chewed her lip and stared straight ahead. She looked like she was trying to decide if she was going to tell him the truth or not. But if it impacted her work for the lodge and its residents, he needed her to be honest about what was going on. It was the only way they would be able to support her.

She knew that better than anyone, having worked as the resident psychologist for as long as she had. If her clients weren't honest with her, she couldn't effectively help them to heal and overcome their issues. The same thing applied to her in this situation. Lawson wanted to help her, but he needed all of the information first.

"I don't know what came over me," she admitted in a small voice, shaking her head and getting to her feet to pour herself a glass of water. She lifted it to her lips and took a long sip, swallowed and then spoke again, a little more clearly this time.

"I can't discuss specifics, you know that. But...it was just like any other session," she explained. "We were talking about some of his stuff, you know, and it brought up some triggers for him. He started to get agitated, totally normal for a guy in his position, but when he got up and started pacing around…it—it just pressed some button inside of me. I didn't know how to handle it."

Her face was pale, her normal bright eyes dim, as she recounted the incident to him. He could tell how spooked she was—it probably triggered her flight response. Even though it had been months since everything that had gone down with Jed, she was still clearly carrying the trauma from it, whether she wanted to admit it or not.

"I'm sorry," she told him, finally lifting her gaze to meet his. "I should have… I should have been more prepared for something like that in sessions. It's normal. I didn't mean to freak him out." She sighed, rubbing her temples. "Damn, I feel like I've put our sessions back with this."

"It's okay," he assured her gently. He didn't like seeing her like this. He reached his hand out to touch her shoulder in support, but drew it back and dropped it to his side. He needed to keep his emotions in check and be professional here.

"I don't know what's gotten into me recently." She sighed and closed her eyes, shaking her head.

Lawson cocked an eyebrow. Really, she didn't? It seemed pretty clear to him, even if she wasn't willing to admit it yet. She felt like she needed to be the strong one, always taking care of others and listening to their problems while ignoring her own needs.

Jed Baxter, one of her previous patients, had turned out to be a double agent trying to get close to Xavier, Lawson's business partner, to collect information he was convinced he had. In a session with Sarah, he had smashed up her old office, destroying it right there in front of her eyes. It was a miracle she hadn't been hurt, and Lawson couldn't even imagine how terrified she must have been when it happened.

So, yeah, it made perfect sense to him that she would

struggle with someone else coming at her with the same anger, the same fury, the same harshness. Even if she knew she was safe here, even if she knew that nobody would ever have allowed something like what happened with Jed to happen to her again, psychological wounds didn't heal just like that.

He knew that better than anyone.

"You have nothing to worry about," he promised her. "Why don't you take a break? Go for a walk, get some fresh air, clear your head." He paused and looked her over. "How long has it been since you've had any food? You want to come over to the lodge, get something to eat?"

"I probably should," she told him. "I was running a bit late today. I didn't have time for breakfast."

"Then, yeah, you should," he replied firmly. "It'll do you good to get some food in you. Let's close up and I'll walk you over."

"Thanks," she agreed with a small smile. She flicked her gaze up to meet his, her eyes lingering on his. Like there was something she wanted to tell him—something on her mind she didn't know quite how to put into words.

Whatever it was, she thought better of it, and pulled her jacket from the back of her chair and slipped it over her shoulders. Even though it was warm outside these days, Lawson hadn't seen her without a jacket in several months, almost as though it was a protective layer between her and the rest of the world.

"I'll lock up. I've got the spare keys on me. You have your keys?" He looked over to her for confirmation and saw her pat her pocket, then nod her head.

Lawson got the place locked up, and stole a glance at Sarah out of the corner of his eye. There was something he had been meaning to ask her, something he had wanted to suggest. He hadn't been sure how to bring it up, but he guessed now was as good a time as any under the circumstances. He doubted she was going to take it well, though, but maybe she would come around eventually. He needed to stop beating around the bush and just say it.

"Okay, all set. Let's go." He slipped the keys back into his pocket and placed his hand at the small of her back to get her walking.

"Have you thought about taking a break?" he suggested to her.

She immediately stopped walking and frowned at him. "What do you mean? I'm taking a break right now."

"No, not that kind of break," he replied as he shoved his hands into his pockets.

"So, what, then?" she asked, clearly confused.

He knew Sarah was dedicated to her work; hell, he was pretty sure it was the only thing that was keeping her grounded right now after the attack. But surely, she could see that she wasn't going to be able to help anyone else in a meaningful way until she focused that attention on herself first.

He took a fortifying breath before speaking again. "A longer break," he said. "Take some time to figure things out."

She stood stock-still on the spot. The corners of her mouth turned down into a frown. In her eyes, he could see the shock and it gutted him. This was the last thing she had expected him to say, and he could tell how deeply it stung.

"I'm fine," she said, forced out the words, and crossed her arms over her chest defensively.

He sighed, jerking his head down toward the lodge. "Sure you are, but maybe think about it?" He paused, waiting for her reply. Her frown deepened but she eventually nodded.

"Right now, you still need something to eat," he pointed out. "Come down and get something with me?"

"Fine," she muttered, but the discomfort was evident in her tone. This, he got the feeling, was going to be a problem, but he wasn't going to give up that easily. Just because she was normally the one who took care of everyone else didn't mean that she didn't need someone to look out for her sometimes, too.

Chapter Two

Sarah stuffed her hands into her jacket pockets as she followed Lawson down the path toward the lodge. She felt like an unruly child being put in a time-out for something they weren't truly responsible for. Internally, though, she was reeling. Did she really hear him correctly? She wasn't sure. She felt as though she must be reading in to what he'd said the wrong way, but what else could she take away from his words?

A break. Not just a few hours away, a full-blown break. That was what he had suggested. That was what he wanted her to do. No, there was no way… There was just no *way* she could take that much time away from her work. She would be climbing the walls with boredom.

She had a hard enough time as it was, tossing and turning all night long, replaying the day of Jed's attack over and over again in her head. Given more time to sit with her thoughts, how was that going to make things any better? Be any easier? She would lose her mind.

Besides, this job was her life. This work, it had been her dream since she was a little girl. She had known, even then, that it wasn't going to be easy—known that it was going to demand a lot from her—and she had been prepared for it. She had been aware, from when she had started her training, that it was going to throw some tough situations at her, and she had told herself that she could handle it. She was going to be that safe place, that port in a storm for people who needed it.

"Is this about what happened with Jed?" she demanded, hurrying to catch up with Lawson.

He glanced at her out of the corner of his eye, and nodded. "I just think you could use some time to process it, that's all."

"I don't..." she protested. "I... It only happened a few months ago. I'm still dealing with it—"

"Yeah, and having some space to dedicate to that might do you some good," he replied. "Getting away from here will help you clear your mind, get a better perspective on things."

She shook her head. "No way," she retorted. "I'm fine. I'm just being hard on myself because I was working with him, and I should have seen there was something going on..."

She trailed off, distinctly aware of how it sounded. Like she was still stuck in the process of blaming herself. Hell, if she was, would anyone be surprised? She was supposed to be able to get a good read on people, not—not let a traitor into their midst, a spy who intended to upend the whole place.

She'd always considered herself an intuitive person who could sense the needs and intentions of others. But after what happened with Jed, she didn't trust her own intuition as much anymore. She had let down herself and other people by not seeing through Jed sooner.

Even though the warmth of the summer sun was beating down on her face, she couldn't help but shiver slightly when she thought about everything that had happened. The look on his face when he had gone into a rage in her office, the way his eyes had darkened and his features had twisted into someone who was unrecognizable. The charming smile he had used to deceive them had disappeared.

She'd seen plenty of people working through serious issues before, vanishing into dark memories or bad self-belief, but she had never, in her whole time working as a psychologist, seen a transformation so consuming and so terrifying.

And that—that had stuck with her. Knowing that someone could just flip on a dime like that, go crazy in that way, terrified her. And crazy was the only way she could describe it. The people she treated, they weren't crazy, they were just damaged, trying to navigate the reality of what they had been through as best they could. But Jed? He was deranged…with evil intentions and a darkened soul. And she prayed she was never going to have to deal with someone like that again.

"I can't expect myself to go back to normal that quickly. It takes time," she continued, and she could feel him watching her out of the corner of his eye. They passed Hannah, who offered Sarah a sympathetic smile. Sarah hated people looking at her like that, as though she was some kind of victim, in desperate need of help. She was fine. She just… needed a moment of fresh air and something to eat, that's all.

"Sarah, there's nothing wrong with taking a break," he remarked to her gently. "How many times have you told that to one of your clients?"

She pressed her lips together. Well, she couldn't argue with that, she supposed. Damn the man! He was sneaky, using her own methods against her. And maybe he had a point, but she didn't want to admit that to him, not so easily, anyway. He offered her a kind smile, but she still wasn't reassured. The words he'd said to her about taking a break were swirling around inside her head and she felt a knot forming in her stomach.

All at once, Lawson stopped in his tracks and reached into his pocket. Checking his phone, he frowned, and glanced over at her.

"I have to take this," he told her apologetically. "We can talk more about this later, okay? Please make sure you eat something soon and get some fresh air."

"Yeah, sure," she replied, though she secretly hoped that he was going to forget they'd had this conversation. She knew she should take his concern to heart, and truthfully, she probably did need some time off. She just couldn't entertain the thought of that right now. She needed her work and this place to help keep her grounded right now.

She was proud of what she did here, helping people to find their balance, their footing again. She felt that canceling therapy sessions or shifting her clients to someone else in town would do more harm than good. She needed them as much as they needed her right now.

"You sure you're okay?" he asked her, lingering for another moment before he left.

She nodded, forcing a confidence she didn't quite feel. "I'm fine," she assured him. "You go. Your text seems important."

He paused and looked her over, seemingly trying to gauge the truth in her words. Her skin tingled from each place his gaze landed, but then he nodded and headed back inside the lodge. She hoped it wasn't anything serious. God only knew that this place had been through enough as it was.

"Hey, you want to give me a hand with these flowers?"

Sarah turned to see Hannah sitting back on her heels, a smile on her face. Sarah couldn't help but return it. Hannah always had the brightest, bubbliest energy, especially when she was outside working on her flower beds. She was so proud of the blooms she had managed to bring out this summer, and Sarah could hardly believe that time had passed so quickly as to see them in full bloom like this.

"Is everything alright?" Hannah asked her gently, nodding back up toward the office. Sarah pulled a face. She didn't really want to talk about it again—she felt raw and exposed enough from Lawson's comments. She couldn't really talk about it, anyway, not with Toby being a client.

She knew Hannah had seen how he charged out of her office like his ass was on fire, though he had every right to be upset with her. The moment his triggers had kicked in and he'd started getting agitated, Sarah had started to panic. She'd withdrawn into herself and flashed back to Jed. She hated how scared she'd become when he had started pacing her office floor, clenching his fists at his sides. She'd felt useless, like all her training had suddenly vanished in a puff of smoke, and she had no clue what to do to calm him down.

Him seeing her frozen and pale, with a shocked look on her face hadn't helped, either. He'd given her a look of disappointment and then stalked out the door. This was her job, the one thing she was good at, and she'd failed him. Failing herself and the lodge in the process.

"Sorry, it's a doctor-patient thing. It doesn't matter, anyway," Sarah muttered, trying to shut down the conversation before it went any further. She knew Hannah was just trying to help, but it was hard to see it as anything other than prying into her private business.

"I wasn't talking about the client-thing, Sarah. I meant you. And you matter to me," Hannah told her, crossing her arms over her chest and hitting her with a serious look. Damn, at times like these, she really reminded Sarah of Lawson.

Hannah and Lawson carried themselves with the same seriousness, like they were ready and willing to take on the world given the chance. And neither of them was going to let Sarah get out of this situation without sharing the truth of what was going on in her head. Sarah pulled out the band from her hair and ran her fingers through the curly blond strands.

"I just… I feel like I've been floundering lately," she confessed. "After what happened with Jed, I mean. I thought… I felt confident in myself and my abilities, and now, it's like the ground was ripped out from under me and I've been sinking in quicksand. Like the ability to do my job and the security I've always known here are suddenly gone, you know?"

"Yeah, tell me about it," Hannah agreed, her brow furrowed. "It screwed me up for a while, too."

"I'm sorry to hear that," Sarah replied.

Hannah cocked an eyebrow. "Hey, we're not talking about me right now," she reminded her. "We're talking about what's going on with you. You could take some time off, you know, figure out how to handle it."

Sarah closed her eyes and sighed. "That's what Lawson said. I don't want to leave my patients like that," she remarked, shaking her head. "I don't think it's a good idea. They need stability and continuity for their treatment to really work, and that's not going to happen if I just vanish off the face of the earth."

"Yeah, but they're not going to receive proper treatment from you if you're freaking out all the time, either," she pointed out.

"I know, I know," Sarah conceded. "I feel like I'm more like my patients than a therapist right now. Normally, I'm in control, but now, I just don't know how to handle myself."

"You should consider seeing a therapist yourself," Hannah suggested. "You could find someone in town, I'm sure of it—"

Sarah shook her head again. She knew it was likely a good idea, but there wasn't a chance in hell that she was going to up and leave the lodge high and dry like that. Plus, what would it say about her and her ability to help others if she ran away? This was her job and Warrior Peak Sanctuary was her home. She wasn't going to be run off by her own insecurities. She'd find a way to deal with them.

"I just need to think about this logically," she replied. "I have all the skills I need to get this under control, I just have to find a way to implement them. Grounding exercises, breathing control, stuff like that. Techniques I'd suggest to my own clients."

She could sense the doubt in Hannah's mind before she even made eye contact with her, but she didn't want to deal with it right now, not when she had already been dealing with her own traumatic issues. Hannah was doing much better in her struggles. Sarah had seen tremendous improvement in her. She didn't want to set her back by pulling her into her own mess.

She was telling the truth, after all. She knew exactly how to work through trauma, at least on a technical level. She had served as the touchstone for so many people who'd come and gone through Warrior Peak's therapy program. People who'd relied on her for support and help in their hardest, darkest times. Why couldn't she just...do the same for herself now, too?

Maybe she just needed more exercise. Take a look at her diet, make sure she wasn't getting too much caffeine, which could be putting her on edge. There were plenty of steps she could take before she would have to look elsewhere for help, and she was determined to do everything she could to focus on them rather than allow herself to get involved with something outside this place.

"So, need help with the flowers?" she asked, nodding to the beds in front of them, trying to change the subject back to Hannah's initial question.

Hannah glanced down at them, as though she had almost forgotten they were there. "Sure, but I don't want to interrupt you getting something to eat."

"No, I'm good. I don't think I could eat right now, anyway."

"Then, yeah, I could use some help. But let me know if you change your mind about eating," she added, handing her the shears.

"You've done such a good job with these," Sarah remarked, shifting the conversation to something else. The more time she spent focused on her freak-out in Toby's therapy session earlier, the more likely it was that it would turn into harmful rumination, and she really, really didn't need that right now.

Hannah brightened up as soon as she mentioned the flowers.

"I know, right?" she replied proudly. "I thought it would take more for them to bloom this first time around, but I guess I have a green thumb."

"You do," Sarah agreed, and she stooped down to smell the peonies. Their sweet, rosy perfume filled the air around her, and she closed her eyes, trying to ground herself with a focus on the scent.

See? I'm fine.

She just needed to give herself a little more time, and focus her energy on the grounding and calming techniques she would have prescribed to any of her clients, and she would be back to normal in no time.

At least, that was what she had to keep telling herself. Because the thought of having to leave this place, for anything at all, was more than a little terrifying to her right now.

Chapter Three

Lawson strode down the main hallway in the lodge with purposeful strides. He went past Reception and the main gathering room, and was passing the dining hall, where he heard someone call his name.

"Hey, Lawson!"

He glanced around, and saw Xavier and Cade hanging out by the dining table in the center of the room, clearing out the plates from the recent meal.

"Can you give us a hand with all this?" Cade called to him. "Aaron's out at the paddock and we could use an extra pair of hands."

Lawson held up his phone and made an apologetic face. "Sorry, guys. I have to take this," he told them.

Xavier shook his head at him. "Anything to get out of dish duty, huh?" he teased.

Lawson held his hands up. "You got me," he joked. "See you guys in a bit."

Truth be told, he didn't have time to stick around and help out right now. No, he'd just gotten a text from someone he hadn't heard from in a hell of a long time, and something told him that if she was getting in touch with him, something had to be going on. Something bad.

The text from Lainey Daye had told him to get to somewhere he wouldn't be overheard and call her. He knew she wasn't screwing around or being overdramatic when she'd typed that, either. Lainey had never taken a joking attitude. She always said exactly what she meant, and nothing more.

It was one of the many things that had made her such a good agent for the CIA. Lawson had trained alongside her, and she had worked in the agency for the better part of a decade before she'd left field duty and begun working as an analyst instead.

The two of them had kept in touch on and off, though they had mostly been focused on their own lives the last few years. Still, Lawson felt some loyalty to her, same as he was sure she did to him, and he wasn't going to leave her out in the cold if something was going on and she needed his help.

He reached his room and pulled the door shut behind him, double-checking to make sure it was locked. He dialed her back and lifted the phone to his ear, and it rang a couple of times before Lainey answered.

"Lawson?"

"Lainey. I'm alone," he told her. "What's going on?"

"Good," she replied, her voice taut.

Lawson could tell at once that something was up, and he didn't like it. They'd worked together for long enough that he could recognize when something was wrong, and when it came to Lainey, he knew it wasn't going to be anything simple. She had a knack for diving in headfirst when it was something important to her.

"What's happening?" he demanded. "Are you safe?"

"For now," she replied. "Can you meet me in town? I don't want to say much over the phone."

"In town?"

"I'm at a café, not far from the sewing shop," she explained.

He frowned. “Wait, you’re…”

“Yes. It shouldn’t take you more than an hour to get down here,” she replied. “Can you make it? I need to talk to you. In person. It’s really important.”

“Of course I can,” he replied without even really thinking twice about it. He was never going to leave Lainey out in the cold, and if she had come all this way to find him, she must have believed he was the only person who could help her. “I’ll need to shift a couple things here, then I’ll be on my way.”

“Good,” she responded. “Please, hurry. I’ll see you soon, Lawson.”

And with that, she hung up, leaving him even more confused than before. What the hell was happening? Why was she here? Why didn’t she just come up to Warrior Peak? He needed to get moving if he was going to find out.

As he gathered himself, his mind drifted back to their time together in the agency. They had worked together well, their last mission a drug bust in Richmond that went off without a hitch. With both of their analytical minds in the game, they had managed to put together a plan that led to no casualties, the drug runners arrested and their stash in police custody, where it belonged. They’d gotten a hell of a lot of dangerous trash off the streets that day, and he was still proud of that.

Afterward, they’d gone to get a beer together. Well, he’d had a beer. He’d noticed at once that she wasn’t drinking, and had wondered aloud what was keeping her from her usual postwork celebration. They had grabbed drinks together multiple times over the years and it wasn’t like her to just order water.

“I—I’m pregnant,” she’d blurted out.

His eyebrows had nearly vanished off the top of his head. "What the hell?"

She looked up at him, and he could see how torn she was, the pain written all over her face.

"I can't do this anymore, Lawson," she admitted. "I… This work, it's getting to me. I used to love the high I got after a job well done. But now, I have other things to think about. Other priorities, the baby…"

Lawson was stunned. She hadn't even told him she was seeing anyone, and now she was pregnant? Sure enough, though, that was the end of it for her. She wanted to leave fieldwork and focus on raising her kid with the love of her life, and he couldn't blame her.

Doing what they did, day in and day out, was tough on families, and he'd heard of way too many people who'd ended up divorced because of the amount of pressure their line of work had put on them. Lainey could see it just as clearly as he could—she would have to make a choice. And she chose her new life.

Of course, Lawson had missed her, but he wanted the best for her, and he trusted that she knew what that was. She had retired from the field to start working as an analyst, a much safer job with more manageable hours. He had asked about her in their mutual circles a few times over the years, and based on the small details he'd picked up, she seemed to be doing really well.

But this? This wasn't good. This sounded serious. What had happened to throw her back into the middle of the action like this? He knew she wasn't in town just to catch up with an old friend. Hell, she could just come up to the lodge for that.

His mind was spinning as he tried to put the pieces together, but he knew there was no point in guessing until he was in front of her and she could tell him herself what was going on.

He left his room and headed down to the entrance as he tried to keep his thoughts from running wild. She had said she was safe for now, so someone was chasing her? Looking for her? For what purpose? Information, or something worse?

He was starting to give himself a headache but he couldn't seem to stop the questions from forming in his mind. What had happened to her kid, her husband? He knew how much they meant to her and he doubted she would have been able to handle it if something had happened to them. Damn, the thought of it made the hair on the back of his neck stand up.

He'd learned what it was like to have the things he held close threatened these last several months, and it wasn't a good feeling.

He diverted down one of the side halls and headed downstairs. He knew he needed to let Xavier know he was leaving the property and what little he knew of Lainey's urgent request. They were business partners, but they were also best friends and they looked out for each other in all ways.

"Hey," Lawson said as he walked in the office door. Xavier glanced up from the papers on his desk, his brow furrowed. A far cry from the goofy guy clearing dishes just ten minutes ago.

"What's up?" Xavier asked, narrowing his eyes. "Everything okay?"

"Everything's fine," he assured him, even though he didn't know if it was truly the case. "I'm going down to Blue Ridge for a bit. I got a call from an old friend at the CIA. Remember Lainey Daye?"

Xavier's shoulders immediately tensed at the mention of the CIA. Lawson didn't blame him after everything that'd gone down a few months prior. "Yeah, didn't work with her, but I remember her. What's going on?"

"I'm not sure yet—she asked me to come meet her. Can you hold down the fort for now?"

"You got it," Xavier replied with a nod. "You need help? Backup?"

"Not right now," he answered, slipping his hands into his pockets. "I'll keep you updated as much as I can. But I need to go, it seemed pretty urgent. I'm not sure when I'll be back, either, probably later tonight."

A dark shadow flitted across Xavier's face, and Lawson could tell his mind was drifting back to the memories of what had happened with Jed just a few months ago. He'd blamed himself for that, for bringing that kind of danger to their door, even though Lawson had tried to tell him he had nothing at all to feel guilty about.

Everyone came to Warrior Peak with some history to their name, and sometimes, that history came back to bite them in the ass. It wasn't Xavier's fault that a deranged man was desperate for information about illegal weapons and would stop at nothing to get it.

"Oh, and can you keep an eye on Sarah for me while I'm out?" Lawson asked.

Xavier cocked an eyebrow. "I guess so," he replied. "Why, is something going on with her?"

"Something happened in her last appointment," Lawson explained. "She should be okay now, but she seemed pretty shaken up by it. I don't want her getting into her head about it, you know?"

"You got it," Xavier agreed, and Lawson nodded his gratitude before he turned to head out to his truck.

Even though the sun was shining above his head, he felt a shiver run down his spine. Lainey reaching out to him like this wasn't exactly what he had expected. As far as he knew, she was living a quiet life as an analyst and enjoying her family life. Something told him that she wouldn't have been contacting him unless she felt as though she didn't have any other choice. When she had gotten out of the game, she'd been intent on making a new life for herself, a life that didn't revolve around the stress and danger of what she'd known before.

But, as he knew all too well, just because you wanted to leave something behind, it didn't mean it wasn't going to come looking for you at some point or another. So if he could help her get through this, then he would.

He owed her that much.

He jumped into his truck and pulled away from the sanctuary, watching the main building shrink in his rearview mirror. And he said a brief prayer to whoever might be listening that whatever was going on with Lainey didn't cause any more trouble at Warrior Peak.

Because God only knew they had been through enough lately as it was.

Chapter Four

Sarah took a deep breath as she hovered in the doorway to the dining room. This should have been a calm, relaxing part of her day, a chance to unwind with the people she cared about, and catch up with others about things going on at the lodge.

Instead, she knew she needed to talk to Toby after what had transpired earlier in his therapy session. The way she had reacted had been so unprofessional and she felt awful about it. He had every right to be upset by her behavior and she needed to make things right. She didn't want to be the cause of a setback in his recovery.

Smoothing down her skirt, Sarah walked over to Toby, who was serving himself up a generous portion of mac and cheese from the large pot on the table. He glanced over at her as she drew closer to him, and she could see the annoyance on his face. She didn't blame him. He'd come to her for help, after all, and she had freaked out on him. He was perfectly within his rights to be annoyed or angry at her for what had happened.

"Hey, Toby, do you have a minute?" she asked him and glanced around, making sure no one else was approaching. She wanted to apologize to him but she didn't want everyone else to know what was going on.

He sighed and put down his plate, turning to face her. "Sure," he replied. The current residents at Warrior Peak were a small enough group of people that, if someone wanted to talk, it was better to just get it over with and have a conversation with them. It was useless to try to avoid them, and he knew that as well as anyone.

"Thanks," she murmured, and she twisted her hands into a knot in front of her, trying to remember what she'd practiced in her head before she'd come over. "Um, I wanted to apologize about what happened earlier," she explained. "In your session."

"Right," he replied, eyeing her with obvious doubt.

She took a deep breath, and forced herself to keep going. "When you got emotional," she continued. "It triggered something in me. And I know that's not fair. I know you come to me for help because you want guidance and to work through everything that's happened to you. It's not your fault that some of what we were talking about brought my unpleasant memories to the surface."

She realized she was rambling, and slowed herself down, taking a deep breath, trying to ground herself in the moment. The smell of the food around her, the chatter of people filling the room. See? She was okay. She could do this. She wasn't going to start freaking out again, not a chance in hell.

"It triggered my flight response and that's why I shut down like I did," she went on. "I had a panic attack, and I know that's not helpful for you in the work that you're doing. I should have been able to handle my own triggers better, but I need you to know that they had nothing to do with you. It was all on me. Your emotions are completely valid, and I apologize for how I reacted."

He nodded slowly. She could see some of the doubt and

irritation starting to edge away now that she had explained it to him.

"I know that wasn't an appropriate interaction for us to have as a patient and a therapist, and I understand completely if you'd like to seek care elsewhere," she said. "There are a few great therapists I can put you in touch with if that's how you'd like to move forward. But, if you're willing to give me another chance, I would love to pick up where we left off."

Finally, a smile crossed his face, and he shook his head. "I don't want to work with anyone else," he replied. "I'd like to keep working with you, Sarah. If you think it's going to be okay for you."

"It will be," she promised him, a flood of relief washing through her. She wasn't sure how she would have felt if he had accepted her offer to set him up with a new therapist, but she was relieved he was willing to let her try again. He clearly had some level of trust in her, despite how messy things had gotten before.

"Thanks, Sarah," he told her. "Now, if you don't mind, I want to have some dinner."

"Of course," she replied. "Don't let me stop you."

And, as she stood there, she realized that her stomach was grumbling. After the messed-up session and the way the rest of her morning had gone, she'd lost her appetite. But now, it seemed to be coming back. The food smelled so good.

She grabbed herself a plate and started to load it up, and then went to join the rest of the staff sitting with the current guests at the long table that ran down the center of the dining room.

She slid in next to Hannah, who was sitting beside Xavier, as she always was these days. Opposite her sat Aaron, and then Cade and River, who were chatting about something that caused River's cheeks to flush. Sarah smiled at the love that shined brightly from the couple. They deserved it after what they'd been through the year before at the lodge.

There were a couple of people missing, though. Bailey would still be down in Blue Ridge finishing her shift at the police station, but Lawson seemed to be absent. That was unusual. Sarah glanced around, wondering if she was missing something, but if she was, she couldn't figure it out. Maybe he had just gotten called away for something more important than a meal?

She tried to focus on the food in front of her, not letting her mind wander off in too many directions. Her thoughts drifted back to the text he'd received. Hopefully, it wasn't bad news and Lawson was just busy with something around the property. She'd have to catch up to him later.

She wanted to check in with him, though, and tell him that she'd smoothed things out with Toby and that he still wanted to work with her. That would prove that she didn't need to take a break, right?

Sarah ate quietly, glad to just be surrounded by people she knew she could trust. She was starting to feel a whole lot better compared to the mess that she was earlier in the day and she could almost convince herself that she was already putting it behind her. That was what she had to believe, anyway.

"Yeah, I mean, I've seen it reported in a couple of places..."

Sarah turned her head to tune in to the conversation happening down the table. Kieran Abbott, one of the new arrivals, had his brow furrowed as he recounted it to Xavier, sitting next to him.

"And how many people did you say had gone missing?" Xavier asked, sounding concerned.

"I think it was a half-dozen women in the last few

months," he replied. He pulled his phone out of his pocket and tapped it a couple of times to pull up an article. "Yeah, look. This is the piece I saw on it…"

Kieran handed his phone to Xavier, since he was in the center of the group chatting. Everyone close leaned in to get a better look at what was written on the screen in front of them. The article, it seemed, covered a spate of vanishings along Highway 50—one of the roads that ran by the Warrior Peak Sanctuary. The highway ran from California to Maryland and was a primary state highway in North Carolina; actually, it was known as NC 50 there.

The pictures of the women who must have been among the missing, looking innocent and free, smiled out from the screen.

"I had no idea," Hannah muttered, and Sarah could hear the fear in her voice. They had all seen so much darkness, so much pain this last year or so, it must have been hard for Hannah to hear about something like this. Sarah gave her hand a quick squeeze under the table, silently comforting her.

"Yeah, I saw it covered in a few places," Kieran replied with a shrug as Xavier handed his phone back and Kieran tucked it back into his pocket. "A bunch of women have gone missing along that road. I don't know if they think it's the same person, or maybe just the weather that's taking them out, but…" He trailed off, leaving the possibilities hanging in the air.

"Isn't there a section of it somewhere called the loneliest highway in America?" Hannah remarked. "I mean, if someone was going to pick a place to hunt for vulnerable women, that would be the one to go for."

"That's Nevada actually. But, I agree," Xavier added. "It's still pretty secluded up in these mountains. Not a lot of places to stop on the winding roads. It could just be the weather, but the fact that it's mostly women going missing…it sets off my alarm bells. I'm going to do a little research, see if there's anything else going on that we might not know about."

"I'm sorry for bringing the mood down," Kieran replied, shaking his head. "I just thought you guys should know."

"No, it's good for us to know," Xavier assured him. "We'll be extra careful from here on out. Keep an eye out for any women traveling by themselves, and make sure they're safe. If they're planning on coming here to the lodge and they're alone, maybe offer them lifts so they're not driving alone."

Sarah glanced over to River, whose face had paled. Cade had found River on the side of the road not too far from there, and Sarah could tell from her expression that she was pondering the possibility of what might have happened if she hadn't been so lucky as to meet him. Would she have ended up being a target? The thought of it made Sarah's stomach twist into a knot. She had become so fond of River since she had arrived here, and the very idea of her getting hurt was more than she could take.

"Everyone, keep your wits about you if you're out there by yourselves," Xavier added, looking around the table. "It's probably nothing, but I don't want any of you getting hurt."

The conversation moved on, as Hannah shifted to something more upbeat—talking about her flower beds and the horses. Soon enough the dour faces turned into smiles, and laughter carried through the room. Leave it to Hannah and her bright personality to turn things around.

Soon, dinner was through and Sarah hung around to help Xavier clean up. As they were collecting and stacking dishes, her skin started to prickle. She could feel him watching her.

"How are you doing?" he asked her. "I saw you talking with Toby earlier."

She sighed, and glanced over at him. "Did Lawson tell you talk to me?"

"He told me to keep an eye on you while he was out."

"Where is he, anyway? I haven't seen him since this morning," she asked, frowning.

"Running errands in town," he replied vaguely. Did he know what Lawson was really doing, or did he just not want to tell her? Either way, she knew that was all he was going to say.

"Okay, well, I'm fine," she replied firmly. "I don't need Lawson telling everyone else my business—"

"He wasn't telling me your business, Sarah," he said, shaking his head like he was disappointed in her that she thought that way about Lawson. "He was just worried about you. Wanted to make sure you were doing okay, that's all."

Now, she felt properly chastised. "I'm okay," she sighed. "I… It's just been a difficult few months, that's all."

"I know," he agreed. "It has been for all of us. But you know you can always speak with one of us if it's getting to be too much for you, right? You don't have to keep it to yourself. No one will fault you. Everyone needs a helping hand now and then."

"I know," she responded, and she managed a smile. "Thanks, Xavier. I'm alright. I needed to clear something up with Toby, but everything's good now."

"You're a great therapist, never doubt that," he told her. "He's lucky to have you. We all are."

She smiled again, this time more sincerely. "Come on, stop trying to butter me up and let's get these tables cleaned," she said playfully, and they began moving the dishes to the kitchen, where River and Hannah were on wash-up duty.

When they were all done, Xavier headed down to the office to finish up some work he'd started before dinner, and Hannah and River walked Sarah back toward her little cabin. It was nothing special, but she enjoyed it much more than the room she stayed in at the lodge. She was glad to have a place just for her, that she could call home.

"It's such a beautiful night," Hannah remarked, tipping back her head to catch the last rays of the sun before they dipped behind the mountain.

"It really is," Sarah agreed, and she glanced over at River. She could tell just from the look on her face that she was preoccupied with the conversation they'd had earlier, about the missing women.

She nudged her gently, pulling her back into the moment. "You okay, River?"

River blinked, and then nodded, wrapping her arms around herself. "I'm fine," she assured them. "I just… I can't stop thinking about those poor women who went missing. It could have been me, if Cade hadn't been there to find me."

"But it wasn't you," Sarah reminded her. "You're okay. You're safe here."

"I know." River sighed, kicking at a loose rock on the ground as they walked. "But—but so many of those women weren't. It doesn't feel fair, you know?"

They reached Sarah's cabin, and she paused, looking at River with a concerned furrow in her brow. She could tell when her friend was struggling, and it was obvious from the look on her face that she was having a hard time holding herself together right now.

"Xavier said he's going to look into it," Hannah reminded her. "If there is anything going on out there, we'll know about it soon enough. And then we can handle it. Right?"

"Right," River agreed, though she sounded far from sure

about it. Sarah unlocked the door to her cabin, but before she stepped inside, she felt a cold shiver run along her spine.

She wasn't sure what it was, but all this talk of what had been happening with those missing women had her feeling out of sorts. She couldn't put her finger on exactly what it was that was going through her head right now, but she knew she didn't like it.

And she knew, all too clearly, that it reminded her of what she had felt when she had been sitting opposite Jed in those therapy meetings. And look at how that had ended.

"Anyway, you should get some rest," Hannah told her, leaning over to give her a hug. "I'll see you tomorrow."

"See you tomorrow," Sarah returned, trying to match Hannah's bright smile. She didn't want to be a downer, and she didn't want it getting back to Xavier or Lawson that she seemed twisted up about anything, either.

Or else they were going to make her take that break that she wanted to avoid more than anything in the world. And the thought of giving up—or even taking a break from—her work, the one thing that was keeping her distracted right now, was more than she could bear.

Chapter Five

Lawson sat opposite Lainey in Reed's Café, as she clung to a cup of cinnamon-scented decaf coffee like it was a buoy in the middle of a stormy sea. Her gaze darted left and right, and Lawson eyed her with sympathy.

"Nobody's going to come looking for you here," he assured her. "You have nothing to worry about. Okay?"

"I don't know if I believe that," she admitted, shaking her head and chewing her lip.

"You trust me, right?" he pointed out. "That's why you came here in the first place. So, talk to me, Lainey. Tell me what's going on."

She sighed deeply, and he could tell it came from some place deep down in her soul. She was clearly carrying the weight of something enormous on her back, and she was struggling to keep herself upright underneath it.

"I trust you," she admitted. "I just… I've kept all of this under wraps for so long, or at least, I've tried to. I'm not used to talking about it."

"You called me, remember. Talking about it is the only way we're going to be able to help you," he told her gently. "You've got to tell me what you're running from."

She nodded, taking a sip of her coffee. He couldn't help but notice that her hands were shaking. Damn, he had seen her handle a whole lot when they had been working at the agency together, so for something to spook her this badly, it had to be big.

"I came across something strange on one of the recent accounts I was responsible for running a financial analysis on," she explained. "I kept running across this one particular name and the name kept popping up in some unusual places. He wasn't connected to the accounts I was working on, but somehow, he seemed to be paying in and withdrawing from one of the connected accounts, then different kinds of accounts branching out from it."

Lainey took a deep breath before continuing and Lawson sat back and crossed his arms as he processed her words.

"I know it wasn't part of my job, but I started following the different trails and some dead-ended but others continued to branch off into other accounts owned by him or shell companies disguised as legitimate businesses. The man was apparently running several different schemes and had his hands in a lot of illegal stuff—everything bad you could think of, and probably more."

"Were you able to find a name? Or a main account where all the funds were flowing through?"

Lainey glanced at him again and lowered her voice even more. "I couldn't find them all, but I found some. And the man's name is Victor. Victor Granger. He's the head of a big crime ring and runs pretty much everything you can imagine. Drugs, weapons and…trafficking, Lawson. He has all these young women and even girls working for him. He's brutal and sadistic in his punishments and revenge."

His eyes widened and tension ran through his entire body. It didn't surprise him that she had caught on to something like that.

She had always been smart and observant, and able to

spot when something was off. She was the last person he'd want looking into him if he was trying to pull off crimes of the magnitude she was describing.

"So what did you do?" he asked, leaning forward with interest.

"I collected everything I'd found and took it to the higher-ups," she explained. "Presented a case. Told them that we needed to put together an operation to bring him down before he did any more damage than he already had, or hurt any more people. I even offered to organize and lead the operation if they wanted me to."

"And what did they say?"

"They told me in no uncertain terms to back off," she sighed, shaking her head.

He frowned. "Why the hell..."

"Said that I was paranoid and looking for problems where there weren't any because of my past as an agent. Some thought I was actually looking to be in the spotlight," she continued, and he could hear the venom in her voice. She didn't like being pushed off a case for any reason, and this—this sounded big.

"So what are you doing here?" he demanded. "If they told you to back off?"

"When the hell have I ever been good at leaving anything alone?" she pointed out, giving him a wry smile.

"True. You never knew how to back off or to let someone else take over," he replied with a smirk, shaking his head.

"I continued looking into him. He's running a trafficking and kidnapping ring along a highway not far from here, Highway Fifty. His crew is grabbing unsuspected women off the road and he's forcing them to work for him or selling them to clients. I've even tracked a few missing women to a couple of ports to the east and then they've disappeared.

I assumed they'd been sold overseas. He's got twin sons, Lyle and Nelson, who are in on it, too. And he's been getting away with it for far too long. Too many people have been turning a blind eye to it all. I couldn't just sit back and pretend I hadn't seen what I did. Know what I know."

"And, let me guess. He figured out that you'd been tracking him?" he asked.

She nodded. "And it's put a target on my back." She sighed. "And my family, too. That's why I'm here. My tires were slashed, my house was vandalized. My husband took the kids to Florida to stay with his family. I just have to hope that I can keep their attention on me. I couldn't handle if something happened to my family."

Her voice cracked as she spoke, the pain evident. Lawson could see how much this was wearing her down. Her eyes looked lifeless with dark circles underneath, and she appeared a lot older. And not just because ten years had passed. This was something else, something heavier, a weight that she wasn't going to be able to shift from her shoulders until she knew the threat to her family was over.

When she said she wasn't going to be able to leave this alone, he knew she was telling the truth. He hoped he would be able to provide the help she obviously needed.

"This has bad news written all over it, Lainey," he muttered.

"And Granger's not going to take kindly to someone trying to put themselves in the middle of it," she continued. "I know. And I'm sorry to bring this to your door, I just didn't know if there was anyone else I could trust. I can't help but think that there's at least a few leadership in his pocket, or they've at least been threatened by him in some way to just turn a blind eye. I can't see any other reason they'd ignore my information."

"I understand. You were right to come to me," he promised her. "I'll do everything I can to help you with this and to protect you. You have my word on that."

She closed her eyes and leaned back in her seat. "I knew there was a reason I came to you," she murmured, and a small smile crossed her lips. "We always made a good team, right?"

"Agreed," he replied, and he lowered his voice and leaned forward. "So what can you tell me about this guy?"

"Hell, I don't know where to start," she replied. "I think the most pressing thing is the kidnappings he's been doing along Highway Fifty. From everything I've been able to find out about him, he's been laying traps with his goons along the most isolated parts of the roads, and waiting for a woman to come by—hitchhiking, driving alone, something like that—and they offer them help."

"Stopping them someplace isolated like that highway would definitely work. Not a lot around and no one to see or hear anything to report it," Lawson mused.

"Sometimes, they don't even seem to use traps, they just grab them as long as they're alone. Then they sell them off or set them to work doing who knows what. I don't even know what to think about what that might involve. Those poor women."

He grimaced. He was pretty sure he'd heard some talk about women who'd gone missing along the highway lately, and this might explain what had happened to them. The thought of it… God, it made him sick. He'd dealt with a lot of evil people in his time as an agent, but the human traffickers were the lowest of the low, as far as he was concerned.

Abusing the vulnerable to make money, forcing them out into the streets to earn for them… And if this guy was targeting young women, then they could be almost certain that it was sex trafficking, too.

"I want you to pass on to me all the information you have, as soon as you can," he told her. "I'll go through it and see if there's anything we can do. We're in touch with law enforcement here, and I'm sure they'll be willing to help us."

"You think you can trust them?" she asked doubtfully.

He nodded. "I know we can," he replied firmly. "We've worked with them on several cases around the area over the years. And in the meantime, you need to lay low. Have you got somewhere to stay in town?"

"Yeah, I have a room at a local motel," she replied. "It's not much, but it's got what I need to work on this."

"You need to get rid of your phone," he went on. "I'll get you a burner. Let me know the room number you're staying in and I'll get it delivered—"

"Who do you think I am?" she joked, raising her eyebrows. "Of course, I already got rid of my phone. Here's the number for my burner and the info I've got right now." She slid a small piece of paper with her number scribbled on it and a thumb drive across the table.

He grinned as he reached for them. There she was, the woman he had known all those years ago. The badass who would stand up for herself and others and always do what was right, no matter what the world threw at her.

"Of course, you have," he replied. "I'll contact you after I look through everything, okay?"

"Right," she answered, her voice a little shaky, as though she didn't entirely believe that he would be able to help her. He knew this must have been a last resort for her. They hadn't spoken in years, but he was glad she had reached out to him. Especially since it affected the area he now called home.

"It's going to be alright, Lainey," he told her with a confidence he didn't quite feel.

The truth was, he didn't know exactly what they were in for. The last thing he wanted was to bring trouble back to the lodge again. They'd only just finished rebuilding from their last couple of dangerous events—the fire and Jed's destruction.

But when someone came to him looking for help, he was never going to turn them down. That was why he and Xavier had started Warrior Peak Sanctuary in the first place—because there were so many people out there who needed some form of help. They wanted the lodge to be that place, a safe haven where those in trouble could turn to for assistance, or stay.

"You'll get back to your family in no time," he promised her. "We'll bring this Granger asshole and his sons down, and he's not going to have a chance to hurt anyone else. You hear me?"

"I hear you," she replied, and she grinned at him. "Maybe I can introduce you to my kids when all of this is over, huh?"

"Maybe you can," he replied, smiling back at her. He liked that thought. Just because they had both moved on with their lives didn't mean that their friendship couldn't be rekindled. They had been through so much together back in the day. And he'd love for her to meet the others and see the lodge, too.

But right now, he couldn't focus too much on the future. No, he had to think about what was right in front of him, and that was making sure that they did whatever they could to protect her and shut down this crime ring.

Because he would be damned if he let someone else get hurt. He'd seen enough of that the last year or so, and if it was in his power to do something about it, then he definitely would.

Even if going after someone like Victor Granger, someone with the power to scare off the biggest agencies, was probably going to put one hell of a target on his back.

Chapter Six

Sarah closed her office door and turned to walk the short distance to her cabin, inhaling the fragrance of Hannah's peonies on the pathway. Today had been a good day.

A much better day than the one before, anyway. She'd had another session with Toby this afternoon, and though she had initially been a little worried about how it was going to go, it had been far easier than she had imagined. He had been willing to work with her, willing to hear her out, and the two of them actually seemed to get along better than they had before. Like he could see her vulnerabilities now, and had connected to them in some ways, especially after everything he had been through.

Yesterday had been nothing more than an off day, and she was more than happy to leave it behind her for good. On a day like today, it was hard to be in anything but a good mood, with the way the sun was shining down above her. Summer was always the best time of year—the bright days, the long evenings, where you could sit around and talk late into the night without getting too chilly. And, after the year they'd had, they deserved a chance to really kick back and unwind.

She looked up and caught sight of Lawson standing outside the front of the lodge, frowning down at his phone. She could tell even from where she stood that he looked tired. She hoped he hadn't been worrying about her, given how much better she was already doing. She hadn't had a chance to talk to him again since the morning before, when Toby had stormed out of her office upset.

She changed direction and headed over to speak to him, and he tucked away his phone when she approached and met her gaze. She could see dark rings under his eyes, and wondered if he had gotten any sleep last night. She hoped there was nothing going on with the lodge, nothing dangerous…

"Everything okay?" she asked him.

He nodded. "Fine," he replied, his voice a little more curt than she was used to.

She blinked at him in surprise. "I just wanted to tell you I'm feeling so much better," she said, gushing to him. "I had another session with Toby today, and it went really well—"

"I think it'd be good for you to take a break."

She stopped dead in her tracks.

"Wh-what?" she stuttered. "What are you talking about? I just told you I'm fine."

"I still think you could do with some time away from the lodge," he replied. "Let me get you an apartment in town. And a therapist. Somewhere you can really unwind after everything that happened."

She parted her lips in surprise. What was he talking about? First, he had just been suggesting a break, not moving out of the lodge, but now…

"It would do you good, having a quiet place where you could work through your trauma," he continued.

"Trauma?" she asked. "Who said anything about trauma? I've just been having a hard time lately, that's all—"

"Sarah, you know I only want what's best for you. You may not see—or want to see—it as trauma, but that's exactly what Jed did. He terrorized you in your own safe space. It's normal for you to feel uneasy after that. Anyone would. You're a therapist, you know this," he told her firmly, his eyes locking on to hers with a serious expression.

She had no idea what to say. She was completely caught off-guard, and didn't know how to navigate this conversation he'd sprung on her. She'd been so happy with her progress earlier today and wanted to share it with Lawson. Now, he was trying to get rid of her. But why?

"You're just trying to get rid of me," she retorted, practically daring him to argue with her.

He sighed. "That's not what I'm trying to do. I just want you to be safe."

"And I'm safe here!" she protested. "Unless—unless there's something you're not telling me about?"

He didn't reply, letting her words hang heavily in the air. Her eyes widened. *What the hell?*

"Lawson, is something going on?" she asked, her voice shaking slightly.

He shook his head at once, but she could tell from the look on his face that he was lying to her.

"Is someone threatening the lodge again?" she persisted.

"No," he replied. "I'm just… I'm trying to do what's best for you. To protect you."

She locked her eyes on to his, tension strung tight between them. Tension that she tried her best to ignore. Because he was one of the owners of the lodge, and her boss. It would make things way too complicated if something happened between them—even though she truly wanted it to.

But now, as he stood before her, she couldn't help but notice the way his eyes burned into hers. The way his body shifted to be closer to her.

"I don't know how to explain it all to you right now," he told her. "But I will. I promise."

"You better," she muttered. "Because right now, it seems like you just want me gone."

"That's not it at all. Please believe me."

"Then tell me how you really feel," she demanded. She wanted him to acknowledge what was between them. She wanted to know that it wasn't all one-sided on her part. Didn't she deserve that? Or, more to the point, didn't they?

"You know how I feel about you," he murmured.

She shook her head and took a step toward him. The warm air around them seemed to be holding its breath, waiting to see how this was going to turn out.

"I don't, not really," she protested. "You've never told me."

"You're good at your job," he told her.

"And is that it?" she asked. "I'm good at my job and that's why you want to keep me around?"

"That's not what I'm saying."

"No, I can see that," she said. She knew this wasn't fair, this wasn't the smartest way to go about this conversation, but right now, she didn't give a damn. She just wanted him to admit it—to admit what they had been dancing around for months now.

She continued. "You want me out of your hair, so you can, I don't know, focus on someone else?"

His eyes drilled into hers, a flash of anger passing across his face. "That's not true," he growled. His voice dropped, the emotion finally showing. That was what she needed to see from him—the proof that whatever was happening here, it wasn't just in her head. There was something between them. No matter how complicated that might make things.

"So what is true, then?" she asked. "Why are you trying so hard to get me to leave?"

"Because I can't stand the thought of anything happening to you," he responded through gritted teeth. Normally, Lawson was so careful in how he carried himself, but right now, she could see the restraint cracking—she could see him giving in to this feeling between them.

"You're being selfish," she protested. "You just want me gone so you don't have to deal with whatever this could be between us."

"That's not it at all," he replied, moving closer to her, hands coming to her arms, like he was holding her in place. Making sure she wouldn't slip through his fingers. Her breath caught in her throat, and her eyes flicked to his mouth and the stubble across his strong jaw. Her fingers itched to reach out and touch it, to feel it beneath her fingertips.

"Then tell me to stay," she breathed. "Show me that you don't want me to go."

Those words hung between them, almost a dare—she was pleading with him to show her just how much he needed her there. Hopefully, as much as she needed to be there with him. He was the grounding force that had kept her on her feet these last few months, and she couldn't bear the thought of being somewhere without him.

But, instead of speaking, he drew her close to him and pressed his lips onto hers for the first time.

The moment their lips touched, she melted into him. This was what she had been waiting for all this time—his kiss, his promise, the knowledge that he felt this need between them, too. Though they had both pretended not to notice it for the sake of keeping things professional, there was no denying it.

His arms slid to her waist and he gripped her tightly, like

he didn't want to let her go. She reached up, her fingers finding purchase in his hair, the feeling almost surreal after all this time. They were outside the lodge, where anyone could see them, but she didn't care. It felt like the world stood still to give them this moment. It felt right.

When he held her, she felt safe in a way she hadn't in a long time. That sure, strong sense of certainty, knowing that nothing could hurt her as long as she was right here, in his arms. This was where she belonged, whether she had been willing to admit it or not. She was just glad they were finally having this moment between them.

Then, all of a sudden, he pulled back. She let out a small gasp, not ready for it to be over yet. He dropped his hands back to his sides and drew his gaze away from her, as though looking her in the face would have ignited something he knew he couldn't control. She stared at him, willing him to look at her again, to acknowledge what had just happened, but he didn't.

"That didn't change anything, did it? You still want me to go," she demanded, her voice low. Her breath hitched in her throat as she silently begged him to respond to her. She desperately wanted him to say it was all a misunderstanding. That he needed her like she needed him. But the words never came.

Instead, he just stood before her, not saying a word. Her heart thudded in her chest and tears gathered in her eyes, but she refused to let them fall. Not here, not in front of him. She'd shatter later, when she was alone and could process it all.

She was hoping admitting their feelings would change things for the better. They'd be able to move past this bump in the road and be together. But she got it. He couldn't risk having a liability like her around after the way she freaked out at a patient. They had a reputation to uphold and she'd been anything but professional in her behavior that day. He couldn't trust her.

"Fine," she muttered. "You don't have to say anything. I get it. I'll go."

And with that, she turned on her heel and started to march back toward the cabin. The tears were blurring her eyes now, but she blinked them back, not wanting him to see how much all of this had hurt her. She couldn't let him know how long she had been aching for that kiss—or how painful it was to know that it still wasn't enough for him to want to keep her around.

She swiped away the tears as she stepped through the door to her cabin, the pressure of that kiss still lingering on her lips. She had dreamed of kissing Lawson like that for a long time, but she had never imagined she would be reduced to tears after it happened.

Something was off around here; she was sure of it. But, right now, it wasn't her business to stick around and find out what it was. Lawson wanted her gone? She was gone.

And she wasn't going to waste another minute thinking about him.

At least, that was what she had to tell herself.

Chapter Seven

"You've looked over the files I put together for you?" Lawson inquired as he strode into the office where Xavier, Cade and Aaron were waiting for him.

All three of them nodded.

"It's a lot to take in," Cade admitted, as Lawson took his usual seat at the other side of the desk.

"I know," he agreed. "But I want you to be as prepared as possible. Granger's got a serious reputation and the last thing we want is to be walking into this situation without everything we need to know."

"How did you even come across this case, anyway?" Xavier asked, as he leafed through the papers of the file Lawson had delivered to them that morning. He'd called a meeting with the guys, not giving many details at the time, and he was glad to have them here and ready to go. He always felt better when he had a team in place, ready to take on whatever was out there waiting for them. Especially a team like this one.

"It's a long story, but the shorter version is Lainey," he replied, clasping his hands in front of him.

"Lainey. As in *Lainey Daye* Lainey? This is why she contacted you?" Xavier inquired with a furrowed brow. Aaron and Cade looked at the men, waiting for more details.

Aaron spoke up. "For those of us not in the know, who's Lainey?"

"She's someone I partnered with over a decade ago in the CIA—we were good friends. She left the active side of the agency and went on to become an analyst when she started a family. This came across her desk while she was doing research on a case." Lawson rubbed a hand down his face. "It's blown up into a big deal for her, put a target on her back, so she came here looking for my help."

Cade's curt voice cut in. "So she stirred up a hornet's nest and brought it to you for us to help clean it up?"

"It wasn't really her fault—"

"Lawson, seriously," Xavier interrupted. "What you're not saying is she was told to stand down for whatever reason and she kept digging, got herself in trouble." He shook his head. "I didn't work with her, but I remember how she did things."

Lawson sighed. "She didn't do it deliberately, Xavier. If something like this crossed your desk, would you ignore it? It's missing women, trafficking young women, maybe even girls…in our backyard."

"I've been thinking about this since Kieran showed us—and sent Lawson—that article last night. It made everyone at the table uneasy with possible danger so close. I think we should help," Aaron offered. "I mean, our women drive these roads all the time. What if it ended up being one of them? You'd be kicking your own asses or worse if something happened."

Lawson nodded his head toward Aaron in thanks. He appreciated him voicing his thoughts on the matter, because that's exactly where his own had gone. Aaron was a former police officer and engaged to Bailey, who currently worked as a cop down in Blue Ridge. She and the other women there at the lodge traveled to town on these roads all the time. If something ever happened to any of them when the guys could help prevent it…

"What I need to know is whether or not you think you're going to be able to handle it." Lawson directed his comment to the other two men.

Xavier and Cade exchanged a glance. For the first time in a long time, Lawson saw some doubt on Xavier's face.

"Problem?" he asked.

"From this file, this is a large crime ring and this guy sounds pretty dangerous," Xavier remarked. "You sure it's something we can handle?"

Lawson frowned. If there was one person he always expected to jump into a new mission feetfirst, it was Xavier.

"Yeah, I know we can," Lawson replied. "Unless you've got your doubts."

"It's not doubts, exactly." Xavier sighed. "It's just…this guy sounds like seriously bad news and we have no idea how many men he's got working for him. I don't want to bring that kind of trouble here to the lodge. Again. We built this place as a safe haven for people who needed it. To help them recover and find their way after the hell they'd seen and been through. And this place has seen more danger than it ever should have over the last year. We're still recovering from the last. And… Hannah. Now there's something here I know I need to protect."

Lawson grimaced. He should have expected this. Xavier and Hannah had fallen for each other hard and fast these last several months, and Xavier wasn't the guy he had been when they had first started Warrior Peak and the tactical unit. He was more settled now, more focused on what was good for him, instead of what would give him a thrill in the moment.

"I don't crave the excitement or need the adrenaline rush

the way I used to," he continued, gesturing down to the file in front of him. "Justice? For sure. But danger? I don't know if I can handle that again. Or handle putting Hannah in the middle of that. I'm still dealing with what happened last time."

"Agreed," Cade echoed. "This really hit home for River. She's been more unsettled since Kieran mentioned the missing women at dinner. She could have been one of those women. It took her a long time to feel safe again after all she went through and it's brought a lot of that back up for her."

Lawson could see why Cade would be particularly protective of her. A crazed cult leader had chased River hundreds of miles to kidnap her, planning on taking her home to marry him. Cade had actually picked her up hitchhiking on the side of the road on his way to the lodge a few years ago. So, yeah, he understood. Everyone there at the lodge had demons of some sort they dealt with and this would stir a lot of them up.

He got it on a more personal level, too. Because there was someone here he cared about, more than he could put into words. Hell, when she had asked him to elaborate earlier, he hadn't been able to. He could still remember, all too clearly, the way she had looked at him, the pain in her eyes when he hadn't been able to come out with what he needed to say.

He should have told her a little of what was going on. She'd asked if there was danger, and instead of ignoring her question, he should have offered something. Anything, so she'd understand that he was just concerned about her safety, that he wasn't trying to kick her out or get rid of her for good. It was for protection…because he cared and he didn't want her in the line of fire. Knowing what a man like Victor was capable of, if he got his hands on Sarah…

"I don't get why the cops can't handle this, anyway," Cade remarked, interrupting his thoughts.

Lawson shook his head. "That's the problem," he explained. "When Lainey brought this to me, she said she took her findings to the higher-ups and they shut her down. Told her to drop it immediately. She thinks a few might be looking the other way deliberately or involved in some way. Shortly after that, she was targeted. Had to move her family to Florida and she came here for help. She's determined to finish it and she can't go home until she knows her family is safe and the threat is gone."

"And she came to you because you worked together?" Cade asked.

"Because she knows she needs this dealt with by people outside law enforcement," he replied, narrowing his eyes. "And by people who aren't going to get tangled in red tape."

"And you think we can trust her?" Xavier wondered aloud.

"I know we can," Lawson said. "She needs our help. If she could have dealt with this on her own, she would have. But she can't. And if this guy gets to her…" His gut clenched at the thought. He didn't even want to let his mind go there.

Xavier rolled his shoulders back, nodding. "Then I guess we have to do something about it," he said, his voice certain.

"And you agree with her assessment that this Granger guy and his sons are responsible for the women who've been going missing on the highway?" Cade asked.

"It makes sense from the information she collected on the guy. I would be shocked if that wasn't mostly him," Lawson replied. "All the more reason to get this under control. I don't want him operating close to us, when we've got so many vulnerable people coming here. If he picked up someone who was looking to get to the lodge, I don't think

I would be able to forgive myself." He shook his head, trying to eliminate the thought from his mind.

"So how exactly do we move forward with this, then?" Cade asked, flipping through the file on Granger once more.

"We need to get our hands on one of the guys working for him," Xavier suggested. "The file said he had a bunch of guys stationed out along the road. They likely aren't heavily armed or well-defended. It wouldn't be too difficult to shake one of them loose, get them talking to us. I doubt they're all that loyal to him."

"I wouldn't be so sure," Lawson warned. "This guy's got his hands in everything. There's probably no limit to what he'd do to keep his thugs loyal to him. Threaten families, hook them on drugs."

Or maybe that was just what Lawson had to believe. Because if he was honest with himself, and admitted that there were people out there willing to do stuff like that without any good reason, it would have messed with his mind.

"Either way, we can't afford to wait around. Aside from your friend being in danger, think of all the innocent women they've already grabbed or plan to. Our women here," Aaron reminded them.

"We have to find his base of operations in the area, and we need at least one of Granger's guys to give us a location. And we need to do it fast before another woman goes missing," Cade confirmed.

The thought of it set Lawson's teeth on edge. He knew they were right. He still couldn't wrap his head around the fact that this had been going on in their backyard and he hadn't known. It could have continued happening right under their noses and he would have had no clue.

Until it came to Warrior Peak. Until it hurt someone he cared about.

Until it came for Sarah.

He shifted in his seat, turning his attention back to what mattered here. They needed a tight plan, and the guys were right—they needed to act fast.

"Alright, let's do this then. We also need to call Sheriff Willis and go over all this with him when we have an idea of how we're going about it," Lawson declared. "We know for a fact he's on our side, and he'll be aware of the disappearances since it's outside Blue Ridge. We'll need his help officially, if we manage to catch anyone."

They went through the file again, running over every detail to make sure they were all on the same page. It was a lot to take in, Lawson knew that, and he didn't want to risk anything by not making certain that the guys were clear on the task at hand.

They tried to figure out where Victor's base of operations might be, derived from the information that they already had, but there wasn't much to go on. There were a lot of isolated areas up in the mountains where they could be hiding. There had clearly been a concerted effort to make sure nobody could gather too much intel on this guy. Who did he have in his pocket? And how much harder was that going to make their job?

Much as Lawson was trying to stay focused, he found his mind drifting back to Sarah. He couldn't stop thinking about the way she had looked at him before, the pain in her eyes when she had called him out and asked him if he really wanted her to stay.

If he'd had any sense, he would have told her yes, of course, he did, that he needed her here. That he would do anything to keep her around. But he couldn't, not right now, not with everything that was going on.

And now, she was going. He had passed her cabin earlier,

and had seen an open suitcase sitting on the bed, half-filled with her clothes. It had made his chest pang with regret, and he wished he could take it all back, wished he could just tell her how sorry he was and that he didn't mean for it to happen like that, didn't mean for her to actually leave.

Since everything that had gone down with Jed, he had been extra protective of her, and aware of just how vulnerable she was. Aware of just how much it would have hurt if something had happened to her.

When he had seen her right after the attack, the rage he'd felt had caught him off guard. He could normally control himself, even in the most impossible of situations, but with her, it was different. With her, his emotions took control, and he would have done anything to get revenge on the person who had done that to her.

Thinking back to their earlier conversation, he should have handled it better. Told her a little about the situation and asked if she'd be willing to take a short break. Hang out in town and concentrate on herself for a bit. Not make it seem like he didn't want her around. Like he was kicking her out.

He knew it wouldn't have been forever, but *she* hadn't. Not the way he voiced his concerns. When they were done with their meeting, he could seek her out and try to explain. Because if something else happened to Sarah, he would never forgive himself.

But right now, he needed to stay on task. Finish going over the information with the guys and figure out a plan to take down Granger and his crew. Then he'd see where things stood with Sarah. The stakes were too high to get distracted right now.

Chapter Eight

As Sarah stuffed her clothes into her bag, she tried to ignore the women who were standing in the doorway, watching her pack.

"You don't have to just pack up and go right this instant," Bailey protested.

Sarah didn't pay attention to her. She folded up a top with shaky hands, then tossed it into the pile. "Yes, I do," Sarah replied through gritted teeth. "Lawson made that very clear."

"He didn't tell you to pack up and go today, did he?" River asked her.

Sarah paused. Okay, he hadn't said *that* to her. In fact, after the kiss, he hadn't said anything to her. But that had been more than enough for her to wrap her head around what he wanted, and she wasn't going to hang out and pretend like she was fine being in a place she wasn't wanted. "No, but—"

"Then you need to sit down for a second and take a breath," Bailey told her as she put a hand on Sarah's shoulder and guided her to the edge of the bed. "Talk to him. Figure this out. He probably didn't mean it the way it sounded. You know how men can be…"

"Pigheaded?" Sarah retorted. "Arrogant? Mean?"

"I was going to say poor communicators," Bailey replied,

chuckling slightly. "I'm sure Lawson didn't mean it to come across the way it did."

Sarah took a deep breath and sighed.

"I know he really cares about you," Bailey continued, as Sarah put her head in her hands. "There has to be something more to this than what it seems on the surface. He wouldn't just kick you out like that, with such little warning."

"He thinks it's for my own good," Sarah said, rolling her eyes. "So I can recover from…you know, from everything that happened with Jed."

"So he's got the right intentions, then?" River asked.

"Yeah, he just wants you to get better," Bailey told her.

Sarah frowned. "By leaving this place?" she asked. "I don't see how that would work. I don't want to go. This is my home."

Both of the women fell silent for a moment, and then, River cut in once more.

"I don't see why you should have to leave to do that," she pointed out. "I mean, the internet is a thing. You could do therapy online. You shouldn't have to leave if you don't want to."

"My thoughts exactly," Sarah replied, smiling up at River thankfully.

"And, I don't know about everyone else, but I'd miss having you around," River added. Bailey put an arm around Sarah and gave her a squeeze.

"I would, too," she agreed. Sarah leaned her head on her shoulder for a moment, feeling another rush of emotion.

She'd never be able to cope with being away from her friends. The support and comfort she got from them was irreplaceable. She had never felt more accepted and safer than she did there at the lodge. The thought of leaving them and her home, even if only for a little while, made her chest ache. It just didn't feel fair. No matter what Lawson's motivations might have been for trying to encourage her to leave, they felt cruel to her.

"Thanks," Sarah mumbled a little sadly. No matter what they thought about her, if Lawson had decided that she needed to leave, what choice did she have? He co-owned the place, after all, and if he wanted her to take a break, that was that.

She just still couldn't believe he wanted her gone. One little freak-out and he was pushing her out the door. No! No. It just wasn't right. There had to be more to it. She'd worked too hard to get where she was and she wasn't going to let him tell her she had to go. She couldn't abandon all the people who came to her for help, all the progress she'd made with them in their recoveries.

"You guys are right," she told them, suddenly feeling a surge of certainty in her chest. That kiss had thrown her for a loop and scattered her brain, but now she was thinking clearly. Her mind was back on track. She knew what she needed, and she needed to be here; she wasn't about to let Lawson just kick her out. This was her home and she wasn't going anywhere.

"You're going to stay?" Bailey asked, her face brightening.

Sarah nodded with a smile. "I'm going to stay," she replied. "There are too many people who depend on me for guidance and I don't want them to have setbacks. I need to stay busy, too, keep to a routine. I can work on my own stuff while still helping others with theirs, right? I don't have to leave to deal with my own problems."

"Exactly what I was thinking," River agreed. "You've got the right idea."

"Yeah, I don't know why Lawson was trying to chase me

out of here," she remarked, shaking her head. "I work with so many of the residents, what would they have done while I was away? Bring in someone unfamiliar? That could cause other issues and setbacks. Honestly, sometimes, I don't know what's going on inside his head."

River and Bailey exchanged a look, which Sarah noticed at once.

She furrowed her brow and glanced between them. "What is it?" she asked, confused.

"You really don't know, do you?" Bailey asked, with a slight laugh.

"I really don't," she replied. "You want to fill me in?"

"You know, for a smart woman, you can be really dense sometimes," River teaser her gently.

"I have no idea what you're talking about," Sarah protested. "Why are you looking at me like that? What am I missing?"

"You really don't know how Lawson feels about you?" Bailey asked.

Sarah frowned at her. Had she seen the kiss? She hoped not. She felt like she didn't want that exposed to anyone else. She was hurt and embarrassed about what had happened after the kiss, and she didn't want to have to explain all of that to anyone.

"I mean, I know… I guess he… But he wants me gone," she replied.

"He wants to keep you safe," River said gently. "He's protective of you. That's what this is all about."

Sarah shook her head in denial. "I don't know if I can believe that," she muttered, looking down at her hands. It was a sweet thought, him caring about her like that. But if he really wanted her, then he would have told her that after their kiss. Instead, he just stared at her, jaw set tight, unable to come out and say what she needed to hear.

"You should," Bailey laughed. "Everyone else can see it. Including us."

"Yeah, well, until I hear it from him, I think I'll play it safe," she insisted.

She could sense that the two of them were still not entirely convinced by her protestations, and she felt heat rising in her cheeks.

"Wait, you're blushing," River pointed out all of a sudden.

Sarah ducked her head, willing her cheeks to stop giving away her thoughts. She hoped her friends would just drop it.

She should have known better.

"You're blushing because you're thinking about Lawson, aren't you?" Bailey teased.

"No, it's not that!" Sarah protested. "I just… I don't know."

"Did something happen between the two of you?" River asked eagerly, planting herself on the edge of the bed and looking at her expectantly.

Sarah parted her lips, considering what to say. Maybe it would do her good to share what was going on with them, and get it off her chest. These women were her friends, and she knew she could trust them.

"I mean, I guess you could say that," she admitted.

Bailey clapped her hands together. "Okay, now you totally have to spill," she urged her. "What happened?"

Sarah pushed a hand through her curls. She had been doing her best to keep the memory of the kiss from her mind, but having them bring it up like this, it was impossible not to remember the pressure of his fingertips on her hips, the way he pulled her into him like he needed to be as close to her as possible. The way his hair felt between her fingers.

"It was…it was just a kiss," she told them finally, dropping her chin to her chest. She couldn't believe she was talking about this with them. She knew they were going to demand the details.

"Oh, my God, finally!" Bailey exclaimed, tossing her hands up in the air. "I think that means I win the betting pool."

"Tell me you're kidding," Sarah replied.

Bailey laughed. "Yeah, yeah, I'm kidding," she assured her. "But what was it like? Was it everything you hoped it would be?"

Sarah bit her lip. "It was…a lot," she admitted. "It came in the middle of an argument. He was telling me that he wanted me to go, and I was making it clear that I didn't want to leave. We were arguing about it, and I kept challenging him, getting in his face, and then all of a sudden, we were just…kissing."

"Whoa!" Bailey exclaimed. "That sounds kind of hot!"

"It was intense," Sarah said, biting her lip. She remembered the feel of it, the heat moving from his body to hers, like they were silently communicating something between them. She couldn't help but wonder what would have happened if they hadn't been arguing, had just been having a regular conversation, and not in public. Would they have kissed more? Taken their desire in a different direction?

"Did it feel good to get everything out in the open like that?" River asked.

Sarah sighed. "I guess it would have, if it hadn't come in those circumstances," she replied. "I can't figure out what he wants from me, if anything at all. And that kiss, it just made everything way more confusing. It's just such a mess."

"I can imagine," Bailey told her kindly. "But you should cut Lawson some slack. All the time I've known him, he's been friendly but a little closed-off. He's more serious, overly cautious. Of this place and the people he cares about. With everything that's gone down lately, I think it's brought out the more protective side of him. He just wants to keep everyone safe and thinks it's his responsibility to make sure that happens. Not get wrapped up in feelings."

"I guess so," Sarah admitted. "But I feel like I shouldn't have to put up with all this back and forth. If he wants me here—if he wants me at all—he should come out and tell me. Even if he doesn't want to act on it now. I have a right to know and for him to not push me away."

"In a perfect world, for sure," River mused. "But think about everything he's been through in the last year. What we've all been through. It's not that much of a surprise that he would struggle to share his feelings. He might think it would make him too vulnerable to open up like that."

"Yeah, him trying to send you away could be his way of telling you that he wants to keep you close," Bailey suggested.

"And how would that work?" Sarah asked skeptically.

"Hey, I can't read the mind of any man," Bailey protested, holding her hands up. "Maybe you just have to give it time. Talk to him about how you feel."

"And maybe kiss him again?" River suggested.

Sarah couldn't help but laugh. "I'm pretty sure that would just make everything more complicated," she replied. But, at the back of her mind, she felt a tingle of excitement at the thought of feeling his mouth on hers again, feeling his hands wrapped around her, that strong, protective grip that made everything make sense.

"Well, whatever happens, I'm staying," Sarah announced as she started to pull some of her clothes out of her bag. "If he thinks he's getting rid of me that easily, he's going to be in for a surprise."

"Agreed," Bailey replied. "We'd stage a protest if he tried to get rid of you, don't worry."

"Good to know you guys have my back." She laughed, and she got up to give River a hug. Honestly, she didn't know what she would do without these women. They were her family just as much as this place was her home.

Chapter Nine

"I'll catch up with you in the morning, alright?" Lawson told Xavier as they stepped out of his office. "We can figure out exactly what we're going to need to pull this off. And how many favors we're going to need to call in to make it happen."

"Sure. And don't forget the sheriff," Xavier replied. His eyes were filled with certainty and focus. He might have been reluctant to get involved with this in the first place, but now that he was in on it, Lawson could tell he wasn't going to let anything get in the way of seeing this through.

"Right," Lawson confirmed. "After we run through everything one more time tomorrow, I'll give him a call and fill him in on what we're doing. Maybe he can make a few inquiries of his own. That way they won't lead back to us."

It had been a long day of planning. Cade and Aaron had left a short time ago to handle a couple of things they needed to tend to, then go spend time with their women. Lawson and Xavier had continued working on the case, jotting down a few details to follow up on the next day. Afternoon had rolled into evening and now, it was time to take a break. They needed to rest and clear their heads for what was to come. And Xavier was anxious to get back to Hannah, check in and spend some time together.

Which meant there was just one person Lawson needed to speak to now.

Sarah.

She had been on his mind all night, that kiss replaying in his head more times than he could count. More than that, though, the pain on her face when he had stayed silent at her demand to know how he felt about her. He had frozen, torn between wanting her close to him and wanting her to leave for her own safety. He couldn't find the words to express that. Now, he could see how much it must have hurt her, and he would do everything he could to put that right.

Because she was his priority right now. Everyone else on staff at the lodge was coupled up, and they all took care of each other. They could deal with their own stuff on their own terms. But Sarah? Sarah was out on her own, and still struggling with the impact of what had happened with Jed, whether she was willing to admit to it or not. And he intended to do everything in his power to help her.

And sending her away, he could see now, wasn't going to actually do anything to aid her in that task. He was just scared—scared about what might happen if she got caught up in the middle of their takedown of Granger and the trafficking ring. What might happen if she was targeted. That thought was more terrifying than anything else.

Instead of thinking with his head, he'd led with his feelings. That worried him, too. Knowing he cared so deeply for someone to be scared down to his bones for their wellbeing. He wasn't sure how to deal with that. His sister was one thing...she was family. But now, she had Xavier to look after her. But, Sarah... She was something entirely different. He was having a hard time processing it all.

And the kiss.

He wasn't sure what had come over him in that moment.

The way she was looking at him, it just lit a fire inside him—something urgent and demanding he couldn't ignore. Like that might have been the last chance he had to kiss her. And he was sure as hell not going to pass it up.

Normally, at this time in the evening, she was reading a book somewhere outside, enjoying the longer evenings with a glass of wine. Now he didn't know what she was doing. He had seen her at dinner, but she had ignored him, refusing to so much as make eye contact. He couldn't blame her. He'd been an insensitive jerk.

Wandering out to the back porch, he found her reclined on one of the lounge chairs, next to the cold plunge tub. She had a book in one hand and a glass of white wine in the other, condensation forming on the glass.

She glanced up at him, and her eyes narrowed as she laid down her book on her lap. "If you've come to talk to me about leaving, save your breath," she told him. "I'm not going anywhere."

"That's not what I came here to talk about—"

"I'm not leaving my home," she went on, as though she hadn't even heard him. "And before you say anything about the trauma, I've signed up for an online therapist group I got from the recommendation of a colleague I went to school with. The group is going to match me up with a therapist as soon as possible."

"I'm glad to hear it," he replied. "But I don't want you to leave, Sarah."

She stared at him like he had grown an extra head. "But you said…"

"I know what I said," he admitted, shoulders slumping down. "Do you mind if I sit?"

"Go ahead," she murmured, not taking her eyes off him. She seemed to have softened slightly, now that he'd told her he wanted her to stay, and he sank down into one of the seats beside her, wishing he had his own glass of wine to take the edge off this conversation.

"I—I'm sorry about the way I spoke to you," he explained. "I know it wasn't right. I was just trying to wrap my head around some stuff that's been happening around here, and I thought you would be better off somewhere else."

"What's been happening?" she asked, tensing slightly.

He knew he had to level with her. She was perceptive, and if he tried to keep anything from her, she was just going to figure it out in her own time, anyway...and then be even more hurt that he had hidden it.

"We've been presented with an urgent case and we're running a tactical operation out of the lodge," he explained. "The guy we're taking on, he's...a big deal. Influential. And we need to act fast."

Her jaw hung open. "I thought you guys were done with all of that?" she asked, dumbfounded.

"I thought we were, too," he admitted. "But I can't walk away from this one. I have to try to help, if I can. A friend of mine, she's in danger, and the guy who's after her... I can't in good conscience just let him continue on with the level of destruction he's causing. He needs to be stopped so she and others can be safe."

"And what about you?" she asked softly. "Are you going to be okay?"

He straightened his shoulders. "I'll be fine," he replied. "The guys and I are good at what we do. Besides, this is who I am. This is what I've always done."

"It doesn't have to stay that way, though," she whispered.

He sighed. "I don't know about that," he replied. "I just know I have to deal with this. No matter what. I can't let this guy get away. And I just... I didn't want you around when it happened. I thought he might target this place if he gets wind of what we're doing, and I wanted you gone so you wouldn't be in his line of fire if that happened."

"You could have just told me that," she pointed out, but he could see the flicker of a smile on her face. He might not have gone about this the right way, but at least she could see that his intentions were pure.

"I know, and I should have," he agreed. "I should have come clean from the start. I know this isn't my decision to make, and you can't make a choice for yourself unless you have all the information you need."

"Thank you for telling me," she replied, and she reached over to give his hand a squeeze. "Can you tell me anything about this operation? Why it's so important to you?"

"I can't tell you too much," he responded. "There's only so much information we have access to right now."

"I'll take whatever you can give me. I assume it has to be pretty major to have you guys involved?"

"Yeah, this guy's into a lot of illegal stuff. But the main thing we're focusing on are the kidnappings happening in this area," he admitted to her. "They could be related to sex trafficking by this guy and his crew."

The blood drained from her face and she lowered her gaze, clearly shocked by what he'd just said.

"Oh," she murmured. "You think the recent kidnappings off the highway are related to that?"

"We think so," he said. "We're still trying to piece everything together, but it looks likely. We're going to get to the bottom of it, though. We're going to stop it. I promise."

"I know you will," she acknowledged. "I know this is your area of expertise. Sorry for pushing for more information. I didn't mean to overstep."

"It's okay," he assured her, rubbing his thumb along her fingers. "I get it."

"And I'm sorry…" she began, hesitating before she forced the words out. "I shouldn't have put you on the spot and demanded to know how you felt about me." She shook her head when he tried to speak. "You should be allowed to share your feelings in your own way, your own time. And the kiss…"

His eyes darkened at the mention of their kiss and his gaze dropped to her mouth. "Oh, I'm definitely not sorry about that," he replied softly.

She bit her lip, staring at him with hopeful eyes. "Really?"

"Really," he assured her, and he moved closer, kneeling on the porch beside her chair. She was so small, he was at eye level with her right now, and those sweet blue-green eyes were softening.

"I've been thinking about kissing you for a long time," he continued, interlocking his fingers with hers. "I'm just sorry it wasn't how I pictured it."

"It wasn't?" she breathed.

"No, I always pictured it…softer," he murmured. He drew even closer to her, their breath intermingling in the space in front of them.

"You want to show me?" she asked, a smile curling up the corners of her lips.

"If you'll let me," he replied, his gaze burning into hers.

Instead of replying, she nodded and closed her eyes.

So he leaned in the rest of the way, closing the last of the gap between them. Finally, their lips came together again, and this time, it felt far softer, far sweeter.

He reached his hand up to cup her face, and she slid her hands to his arms, holding on to them as though for dear life. He knew just how she felt. There was something about her that felt steady and strong, and as he deepened the kiss, he knew this was what he had been waiting for. Not the two of them, overwhelmed by emotion, but the two of them choosing to give themselves to each other. To accept that want between them, and finally act on it.

His tongue slipped into her mouth as he grazed his fingers down her cheek and moved his hand to the back of her neck to hold her in place. He felt the goose bumps rushing across her soft skin in the process. Her perfume filled the air around them, something sweet and with a hint of vanilla, like fresh cupcakes. And she was just as tempting.

She moved her hand up his arm, sweeping it over the nape of his neck and into his hair, her fingertips digging slightly into his scalp as she pulled him in closer. He felt her touch tingling all the way down his spine, lighting up every inch of his body.

She turned to face him fully, swinging her legs off the lounge chair to the ground. She kissed him harder, her teeth catching on his lip as her book tumbled out of her lap and onto the ground, not giving it a second thought. A damn meteor could have hit the lodge right now, and Lawson doubted it would have been enough to break them apart.

When they finally pulled away from each other, both of them laughed, a tension breaking between them, their argument completely forgotten. For so long, he had done his best to ignore the desire he felt for her, to keep things on a more professional level. But now? This was what he wanted from now on. No hiding. No pretending it wasn't there. Just giving himself over to her, to this desire between them.

"Is that more like you had imagined?" she asked coyly.

"Hmm, much closer," he replied, leaning his forehead against hers. "But I think I need a little more practice to get it right."

She giggled as he leaned into her and kissed her again, the taste of white wine on her lips. He couldn't help but smile into the kiss. He knew there was still so much he needed to worry about, so much he needed to take care of, but right now, all that mattered was how she felt in his arms.

And how certain he was that he would do anything it took to keep her there.

Chapter Ten

Lawson woke with a smile on his face. He was tired and a little stiff from sitting out on the porch with Sarah so long the night before, but it had been worth it. They'd cleared the air and he'd finally told her he had feelings for her. And kissing her… He could kiss her all day and never get tired of her sweet sighs, her pink cheeks and the feel of her skin. She'd made him feel like a teenager again.

It was nice to let everything else fade away and just concentrate on her. On them. Seeing her radiant smile at breakfast made it even better. They sat together, arms and hands brushing as they ate, and conversation flowed easily around them. He couldn't wait for this mission to be over, for Granger to be behind bars, so they could move forward.

After breakfast and cleanup, everyone went to their respective work locations to check in and take care of their immediate duties. Cade and Aaron had a few things to handle around the property while Xavier and Lawson holed up in the office. Xavier had some paperwork to finish up while Lawson spent time on the phone with the sheriff, filling him in on their plan. They had a lot to get done in a short amount of time before putting their plan in motion later that day.

Since the men would be busy all day and into the evening with their mission, the women had decided to drive down the mountain to Blue Ridge that evening for a much-needed break. Lawson was glad to see Sarah feeling better, more like her old self. Having her friends close definitely helped.

After the women left for town, Cade, Lawson, Xavier and Aaron gathered in the office, which had become their war room as they planned their attack against Victor and his men.

Lawson was all too aware of just how much was on the line. Not just Warrior Peak, though that was part of it. Mostly, it was just Sarah. After spending time together last night, his need to protect her had skyrocketed, and he knew he was going to do whatever it took to ensure she didn't have to face any of the trouble this operation might bring to them.

"Are we almost ready to move out?" Xavier asked, glancing around the room. The other men replied with nods. They were all armed, all ready to take on whatever came next. Each of them was taking a different rest stop to keep watch for the comings and goings of Granger's men, and, if the opportunity arose, to grab them before they could do any harm.

Really, it was a reconnaissance mission, but Lawson could tell that the rest of them, like him, were itching to take it to the next level and actually snatch up one of the evil bastards involved in this trafficking.

"It's nearly dark, so we should get stationed at our rest stops as soon as we can," Cade replied.

Lawson nodded in agreement.

Xavier glanced over at him. "You alright?"

"I'm fine," he lied quickly. Truth be told, he'd been worrying a whole lot in the last day or so about what they were getting themselves involved in. Playing back their earlier conversations in his mind, Lawson could understand the others' true fears of setting out on this mission. He didn't want to share his own concerns, though, because he knew that would break the morale.

Even though this was the place he usually felt the most comfortable—working with the guys to come up with a plan to take down someone vile and dangerous—this was more intense than what they had faced off against before, and there was just no avoiding that fact.

Granger was a big fish and capable of bringing down hell on their heads if he decided to, for their interference in his business. One slip would be all it would take to have him and his thugs on their trail.

Then there was Lainey to think about, too. He knew he would never be able to forgive himself if something happened to her or her family because of his failure to act. It made Lawson so mad when he thought of all the people who had failed to lift a finger when she'd brought it to their attention.

But he couldn't let his emotions get the better of him. He needed to keep himself under control. Now, more than ever, there were so many people relying on him to see this through. Not just Lainey, but all the women whom Victor had already targeted and was using and abusing for his business and his own perverse needs, and those still yet to be taken. But not on his watch, if he could prevent it.

Lawson rose to his feet and looked around the room. If there was anyone in the world he trusted to pull off an operation like this, it would be these men in front of him.

"Last chance to back out if you don't want to get involved," he warned them. He wouldn't blame anyone for deciding they didn't want to be part of this. Hell, if Lainey hadn't asked for his help, he wasn't sure he would have put himself in the line of fire at all.

But all three men looked back at him steadily, and Cade answered for the group, with confidence. "We're all in."

None of them wavered for a moment. They really were in—all in.

Lawson nodded back. For the first time since Lainey had brought this to him, he felt hope rise in his chest. They were going to do this.

End Victor Granger's reign of terror once and for all.

AN HOUR OR so later, Lawson pulled his truck to a halt in the desolate rest stop he was using as his stakeout position. The small building was set back from the road, surrounded by thick trees, with a restroom door at each side of the structure lit with a single flickering bulb between them, and a broken snack and soda machine in the center. It was dark and gloomy. It felt as though the whole place was holding its breath, waiting for something to happen.

After killing the engine, Lawson climbed out of the truck and looked around. No vehicles coming either way—this place was empty. An easy hunting ground for anyone searching for women in trouble. He doubted there was CCTV out here, and even if there was, it likely hadn't worked in years, anyway.

Lawson flicked on the warning lights in the truck, a sign that something was wrong and that he was in need of help. He knew that if Granger really had his men working up and down this highway, it wouldn't be long until one of them showed up to check it out. And, when they did, he needed to make it look as though he was a woman.

He sighed as he strung some pearls from the rearview mirror and slipped a pink, fuzzy cover over his wheel. Then he scattered some feminine paraphernalia around the cab—colorful notebooks, a shiny pen, a hairclip, a bright pink backpack and a pair of high heels—where it would be seen. Luckily, he'd been able to borrow some stuff from the women—actually, they all had. The others would be setting up their vehicles like this, too.

Then he got out and leaned a spare tire against the truck and placed a couple of tools on the ground. To anyone driving by, they would think there was a woman in trouble and in need of help…provided they didn't see him.

The trap was set. Now, he just had to wait for someone to take the bait.

He headed over to the restroom and knocked on the women's side, making sure it was empty. When no one responded, he pushed open the door and leaned up against the wall, pulled out his phone and fired off a text to the others to let them know he was in position.

Along the highway, Cade, Xavier and Aaron would be taking up their positions, all of them prepared to snare one of Granger's men as soon as they got the chance. It might not have been the most foolproof plan, but they needed to get their hands on one of the boots-on-the-ground guys to figure out exactly how his operation worked.

Their texts came in one after the other, letting him know that they were ready to go. Lawson glanced out toward his truck, sitting there by the side of the road, and wondered if this had been the right call. He pushed down those thoughts. He couldn't let any doubt get into his mind—he needed to keep a clear head. He knew the guys were all relying on one another to pull this together, and he wasn't going to be the weak link to bring it all crashing down.

Soon enough, one of Granger's men would see a vehicle on the side of the road, broken-down and apparently belonging to a woman. They'd pull over, ready to snatch up another innocent, and instead, they'd be faced with a highly trained ex-cop, former military man, or former agent for their troubles. Lawson hoped they picked his rest stop to come to. He wanted to see the looks on their faces when it happened.

He listened to the road outside. Nothing, just stillness. Damn, he hoped an actual woman didn't turn up looking to use the restroom—it would be hard to explain what he was doing in here if they did.

He needed something to pass the time, to keep himself from overthinking. Then, he thought of Lainey. It had been a few days since he had last spoken to her, and he'd told her he'd update her once they got their plan in motion. Now seemed as good of time as any.

He dialed the number of the burner phone, and she answered a few seconds later.

"Hello?"

"Hey, Lainey, it's me," he greeted her. "How are you doing? Everything okay?"

"So far." She sighed. "What about you guys? Have you had any luck yet?"

"Not yet," he admitted. "But we're working on it. We're stationed along the highway now, all four of us, waiting for one of Granger's men to take the bait. As soon as we have one in our custody, we'll get back to you. We're going to use him to get all the information we can about the man himself and his operation."

"You be careful," she warned. "They're violent men, Lawson. They don't hold anything back. He must do something to ensure their loyalty because they're completely devoted to him."

"I will be," he promised her. "You don't have to worry about us, Lainey. We can handle ourselves."

"I just wish there was more I could do to help." She

sighed. “I hate hiding out here, having you and your friends risk your lives for me and my family.”

“You just focus on staying safe. Stay inside, keep your door locked, keep a look out for any trouble,” he told her firmly. “That’s the most important thing right now. And keep your phone close.”

“I will,” she acknowledged. “I just don’t like feeling useless.”

“You’re not useless,” he assured her. “If you hadn’t brought this to us, we would never have known who was causing all this trouble, right? You’ve given us a break. And now, we can use it to bring these guys down for good.”

“I know you’re right,” she replied. “Just…look after yourselves, okay? I’ll never forgive myself if something happens to one of you for helping me out.”

“No worries, just stay sharp,” he reminded her. “I should go. I need to keep focused on what’s happening here. But with any luck this will all be over soon.”

“I hope so,” she murmured, and he could hear the smile in her voice at the mere thought of it.

“I’ll speak to you later,” he promised her, and they said their goodbyes, leaving Lawson in the quiet of the night once more. He tucked his phone back into his pocket, and pushed the door open another couple of inches. How long were these guys going to make them wait? They had laid out the perfect honey trap for them, and now, they just needed them to take the bait.

When he thought of all the women who’d been lured into this nightmare, all the girls who had been kidnapped and forced into doing God only knew what for that man, it was hard for him to keep his cool. He’d seen a lot of nasty stuff over the years, but this? This might be the worst of it.

But he could handle it. They all could if it meant stopping this criminal organization. His thoughts drifted back to Sarah, their kiss. He had something good going for him now. Lawson knew he'd do anything to protect her, keep her safe. No matter what.

No matter whom he had to take down in the process.

Chapter Eleven

A harried waitress greeted Sarah and the other women as she passed them with a loaded tray of drinks and food. "Welcome, gals. Have a seat wherever you can find one."

"Thank you," Sarah replied, then turned to Hannah. "I'll see if I can find us a seat and you three get the drinks." She nodded toward the bar, then glanced around the packed room before seeing a small group leave a table off to the side by the window, and hurried in that direction.

As she waited, Sarah tilted her head to look at the clear sky above her, lost in thought. The moon was half-full and glowing, not a cloud in sight, and the stars were twinkling in the distance against the dark backdrop of the night. She wasn't sure she would ever get used to being this far out in the middle of nowhere, but it was worth it just for the scenery.

She was startled out of her gazing as Hannah, Bailey and River walked up to their table and set down the drinks.

"Oh, you grabbed a good spot," Bailey cheerfully acknowledged as they settled around the table.

While Sarah and the others reached for their glasses of wine, River scooped up her lemonade. She'd volunteered to be their designated driver for the night, and Sarah was glad she was off the hook and could have a little fun. She wanted to talk to them about everything that had been going on in her head lately, and she knew that she wasn't going to be able to muster up the courage until she'd had a couple of drinks.

"It's a beautiful night." Hannah sighed as she glanced up at the moon above them. Many of the patrons of the bar were sitting outside, enjoying the balmy weather. The low buzz of conversation was comforting to Sarah and she felt like she could finally relax for the first time in forever. She liked knowing that this place was full of people who really seemed to be enjoying themselves, so she wouldn't have to worry about being overheard. She had a lot she wanted to share.

"Yeah, it really is," River agreed. "Shame the guys couldn't join us."

"You know what they're up to tonight?" Hannah asked.

Bailey shook her head. "No idea. As far as I know, they're up at the lodge, making plans for something important."

Suddenly, all eyes at the table turned to Sarah, like she might have a better idea of what was happening.

She cocked an eyebrow. "Why are you all looking at me?"

"Because if anyone knows what Lawson is planning, it's you," Hannah teased her with a laugh.

Sarah felt her cheeks flush with heat. "I don't know what he's up to right now," she admitted. "He did mention that they were going to help look into the kidnappings that were happening around here."

Bailey tilted her head. "You guys haven't talked yet?"

"Not about what they're doing, really," she replied.

"Oh, so about other things, then?" Hannah asked. She always had a nose for gossip, and there was no way she was going to let this go.

"We did clear the air about me leaving," Sarah replied, trailing her finger around the bottom of her wineglass. God, this felt weird. She wanted to share with her friends, but it suddenly occurred to her that she didn't know if she was risking things with Lawson by talking about everything. But she knew she couldn't hide it. Plus, they all talked about their relationships with her and it didn't seem fair to keep hers from them. She wanted to be honest with them and she did need to talk to someone about it all.

"Oh, okay. Now, you have to spill," Bailey announced.

Sarah bit her lip, but couldn't keep the smile off her face. She told them about the kiss they had shared, and how he'd wanted a redo after the way things had gone before.

Hannah made a playful grossed-out face. "Wow, who knew my brother had it in him to be romantic?"

"Holy hell." River laughed. "You guys…you're finally doing it, huh?"

"I'm not really sure what we're doing right now," Sarah replied. She'd hardly allowed herself to follow that train of thought, and had been too spooked at the notion of what might be happening between them to ask more questions about them or go any further than she already had.

Things had been so tense between them for so long, and now, something had actually happened. She felt like one wrong move would be enough to blow it all up, and there was no way in hell she was going to let that happen.

"You're not?" Hannah asked. "You didn't have any type of relationship conversation? Come on, you have to spill. You can't keep us hanging here."

"Hey, it's my love life, not yours," Sarah protested, shaking her head. "I just… I know Lawson has a lot going on right now. And I don't want him to have to drop all of that just because we have feelings for each other or something."

"Not 'or something,'" Hannah corrected her. "You definitely have feelings for each other. It's written all over your faces whenever the two of you are together. I think you two are the last ones to notice."

"Oh, trust me, I did notice signs," Sarah replied. "I just didn't want to push and end up pushing him away. I figured, when he was ready, something would happen."

"And you think he's ready now?" River asked.

Sarah paused for a moment. She hoped he was ready. She wasn't sure she would ever be able to stop thinking about how good their kiss was, or how badly she craved the man. How much she wanted even more.

"I hope so," Sarah responded. She'd been single for a long time now, and she'd be lying if she said she didn't miss having someone special to share her life with. She had done plenty of dating when back in college, but all of the guys she had wound up with had been totally incompatible with her. None of them understood her drive, her dedication to getting her degree or working as hard as she did. They expected her to do what was important to them, not follow her own dreams.

She had stuck with her useless dating life until her PhD, when she'd had to take a long, hard look at herself and accept that she wasn't going to be able to give people helpful advice on their own lives if she was still making the same mistakes in hers. She had sworn off dating, focusing on her career instead, until she was in a place where she could feel confident.

And now, she was. She had a job she loved, was living in a place that felt like home and was surrounded by people she really cared about, who really cared about her. There couldn't have been a better time to start dating again. Not just start dating, though. To build something, with Lawson.

After all this time waiting for the right person to come along at the right time, there were things she wanted to catch up on. Falling in love, building a real life with someone, maybe even having kids, if the time was right.

But that was something for "future" her to consider. She needed to focus on the present, and not put too much pressure on Lawson or herself to jump into this relationship feetfirst. They'd shared a couple of amazing kisses, and that was about it so far, even if the thought of them sent a shiver of delight down her spine.

"I don't want to jinx it," she told the women around her as she shook her head. Hannah opened her mouth, clearly about to hit her with another question, but before she could, a waiter appeared beside them.

"Some drinks," he told them, distributing a few glasses of wine on to the table.

"Oh, we didn't order anything," Bailey remarked, but the waiter nodded over to a table just across from them.

"Those guys ordered them for you," he replied, and all of the women turned around to see whom he was talking about. Sure enough, there were a couple of guys sitting a few tables away, sipping on beers, grinning in their direction.

"Well, I'm not drinking, so I don't want this," River told the waiter.

"I'll take the free drinks!" Hannah replied, grinning.

The waiter shrugged and backed off, leaving the women alone once more.

"You think that's a good idea?" River asked warily. "We don't want to give them the wrong idea."

"They're just drinks," Hannah replied, waving her hand. "It's not like we're accepting a marriage proposal."

"Do you recognize those guys?" Bailey muttered as she stole another glance toward the men who had purchased the drinks.

Sarah shook her head slowly, looking over her shoulder

at them again. They were still watching them as though waiting for a reaction.

"They must be from out of town," Sarah added.

"And they're just trying their luck with some women they thought might be single," Hannah pointed out. "It's not a big deal."

"I don't know," River replied. "It feels…off."

Sarah nodded. She wasn't sure exactly what it was, but there was something nagging at the back of her mind, a warning that something was wrong. In this small town, everyone knew everyone, and it wasn't exactly the kind of place that got a lot of tourists.

"It's fine," Hannah said, trying to assure them. "Come on, it's busy here tonight, it's not like they're going to try anything."

Sarah tried to shake off the doubt in her head. Hannah was likely right. They didn't owe these guys anything for accepting the drinks, right? Maybe they were just trying to be friendly.

The guys kept an eye on them all night, while the women gossiped, laughed and enjoyed each other's company. As the evening wore on, the crowd thinned out, and the women headed back to their car. Sarah noticed the men walking out the door right as they pulled away from the bar.

While driving out of town, Hannah and River chatted about chores that needed to be done the next day at the lodge—guests checking out and vendor calls that had to be made. Bailey chimed in occasionally as she checked her phone for any urgent messages from the police station that required her attention.

Sarah was a little more subdued on the drive, unable to stop thinking about the men who had bought them the drinks earlier. Maybe she was just on edge knowing everything that was going on in town at the moment, but she couldn't help but wonder if there might have been something more to it.

They had been driving on the winding mountain road leading up to Warrior Peak for about fifteen minutes when a pair of headlights flashed in the rearview mirror. Bailey and Sarah were riding in the back and whipped their heads around when the light flooded the back window so they could see what was happening behind them.

"Damn it," Bailey muttered. "There's someone on the road behind us."

River gripped the wheel a little tighter while she glanced in the rearview mirror. Sarah knew she was thinking about the women who had been taken from the side of the road. It was all Sarah could think about, too.

"You recognize the car?" Hannah asked.

"I can't see anything but bright lights," River replied.

Bailey's lips tightened. "What if it's the guys who ordered us drinks?"

"I did see them leave right after us," Sarah volunteered.

All the women exchanged nervous looks. "Maybe we're just being jumpy? You know, from the article and what the men told us at the lodge," River offered.

"Probably. But we're still about forty-five minutes away from the lodge, I'm calling Lawson," Sarah replied, and she dug for her phone in her pocket. She had no idea who was behind them or what they wanted, but she sure as hell wasn't going to sit around waiting to find out. Better to be safe than sorry. As she pulled out her phone, she realized her hand was shaking, and tried her best not to let the others see. She didn't want them noticing how freaked out she was at the situation.

Not until she'd had a chance to speak to Lawson, anyway. He and the others had been in the office when the women had left to go to town. Surely, they'd be done with their meeting by now, right? A couple of the guys could drive down to meet them, and just like that, this whole mess would be over. They would laugh at how paranoid they had been and forget about it. Because there was no way the car behind them could have anything to do with the men Lawson and the others were after right now, they were just feeling out of sorts.

At least, that was what she told herself, as she listened to the phone ring and silently pleaded for Lawson to pick up.

Chapter Twelve

Lawson snatched up the phone as soon as he saw it was Sarah calling and lifted it to his ear.

"You okay?" he asked, concerned.

"Not really," she blurted out.

His heart dropped as soon as he heard the tone of her voice. He knew she would never fool around about something like this. If she sounded that scared, it was because she had a real reason to be, and he hated the thought of her struggling like that.

"What's going on?" he asked, wishing he had somewhere to pace. Right now, in the confines of this restroom, he was stuck in one spot.

"We…we're just coming home from the bar," she told him. "Some guys there had the waiter deliver us drinks. We didn't talk to them and they didn't look familiar, but they left right after us and there's a car behind us on the road right now. We can't help but wonder if it might be them following us."

She paused and took a deep breath, and his gut clenched. *Damn.* Someone was possibly tailing them. Could they be related to the guys they were after tonight? They tended to focus on women driving alone, but he wasn't going to take that chance.

"Listen to me," he told her firmly. "You go straight back to the lodge, okay? Don't slow down and don't pull over. If it is someone following you, they won't try and cross the property lines. Especially if they don't know who else might be around."

At least, he hoped not. Truth be told, he didn't have any confirmation that they wouldn't. This wasn't something they'd anticipated. He hoped that the surveillance there might be enough to scare them off, but if they had come this far, there was a chance they were going to take it even further.

"Okay, we've still got a ways to go," Sarah replied, her voice still trembling. "I… Are you at the lodge?"

"Not right now," he admitted. She let out a small whimper. He hated being so far from her when she was clearly struggling so much, but there was nothing he could do about it.

"Where are you?"

Before he could reply, he heard a noise outside. He cracked the door open and saw a black SUV pulling to a halt next to his truck. Talk about bad timing…

"I'll explain later," he muttered to her, dropping his voice so it wouldn't carry outside the restroom.

"Lawson, I—"

The men stepped out of the SUV—two of them. One of them whistled, calling out to anyone who might have been nearby, and they paced around the truck he'd left there as a lure.

"Listen to me, Sarah," he told her urgently. "Tell Hannah to call Xavier and fill him in on everything that's happening. Do it now. I'll stay on the line with you until you get through."

"Why?"

"Please, just trust me on this," he begged her. "I know how it sounds. Just get her to call him, okay?"

"Sure, okay."

She did as she was told, and, a few moments later, she told him that Hannah had Xavier on the line.

"Okay, good," he replied as he nervously ran a hand through his hair. He glanced outside once more. One of the men was motioning toward the restroom, clearly sensing there was someone inside. "Now, get her to tell Xavier to call all the men back to the lodge. They'll meet you there."

"All of them? Who else is out there?"

"Everyone," he replied. "And tell Xavier that I have our target. I'll handle business while they make sure all of you are safe."

"Target?" she whispered. "Lawson, are you in danger right now?"

"No," he said quickly. "But I'm looking at two guys who are about to be. You have nothing to worry about, Sarah. You just make sure you're safe, okay?"

He hung up before she could answer. He knew she was going to be pissed at him after she found out the details of what he and the others had done, so would the other women, but that was a problem for another time. What mattered was making sure that he pulled this off. They finally had these guys right where they wanted them, and he would be damned if he'd let them slip through his fingers.

He turned on one of the restroom taps, and then dived into a stall, stepping up on to the toilet so they wouldn't be able to see his feet. He wasn't going to give them the slightest heads-up as to what was going on here. There were two of them, after all, and he would need every advantage he could get.

His heart was pounding in his chest, and he wondered

how long it had been since he'd last seen action like this. The adrenaline was rushing through his system, lighting up every part of him, and he clenched his fists at his sides. He was going to make them pay for what they had done, for everything they had pulled on his stretch of road. If he'd known about this before, he would never in a million years have allowed them to get away with it. But this was his chance to bring it to a close.

Or at least, start the process.

"Hello, miss?"

One of the men called out to the supposed damsel in distress as they approached the restroom. They sounded innocent in their inquiry. Helpful. Almost kind. It was a damn good ruse, he had to give them that, even if he hated that they were clearly so well-practiced at it.

The door to the restroom opened. Lawson could see the two men entering through the crack in the stall. He braced himself. He didn't know if they were armed, or what they were packing if they were. But he had the element of surprise, and that had to count for something.

"We saw your vehicle outside. Do you need a hand with a tire change?" one of the guys asked. The sound of the tap running was his only response.

Lawson bided his time. He needed to wait until they were right outside the stall before he made his move. He couldn't risk missing his chance. He couldn't risk screwing this up.

"Check the stalls," one of the men muttered to the other, and they began to make their way along the grimy stalls. First, the one farthest from Lawson, and then, the one next to him.

And finally, both guys were standing right in front of his stall. He planted his hands on each side of it for leverage, as one of them tried the door.

"It's locked," one remarked. "She must be in—"

Before he could finish what he was saying, Lawson swung his legs toward the door with all of his might and slammed his feet into the flimsy wood panel. It crashed off its hinges, and smashed into the two men standing on the other side.

He sprang down on to the floor and quickly surveyed the situation: one of the men had been tossed against the far wall and slammed his head into the dirty tiles, while the other was half-pinned by the door on top of him. He shoved it off his chest and scrambled to his feet, reaching for a weapon at his side.

"What the hell—" he blurted out, but Lawson took advantage of the obvious shock written all over his face. Lawson lunged for the assailant's gun and grabbed it out of his hand, then took his arm, twisted it up roughly behind his back and slammed the man into the wall. The man let out a cry of pain, then Lawson tossed the gun aside and pulled out a pair of cuffs he'd brought with him. He snapped one of them around his wrist and attached the other to a metal pipe hanging on the wall above him.

The other man had gotten to his feet, and Lawson rounded on him. Using the man's dazed state against him, Lawson grabbed his arm, then slapped a second cuff on his wrist before he knew what was happening. There was a wound on the man's head, dripping blood down his face, and Lawson doubted he would have been able to put up much of a fight, anyway, even if he had wanted to.

Lawson pushed the guy back against the wall and lifted the man's cuffed arm above his head, attaching the other end of the cuff to the metal pipe running along the ceiling. He checked the man for weapons and didn't find any, so Lawson pulled out his phone.

While he was dialing the sheriff, he leaned back against the wall and took a deep breath, waiting for the other man to answer. After a few rings, the sheriff picked up, his voice a little groggy.

"Sorry to wake you, sheriff," Lawson greeted. "But I have a couple of guys with me here I thought you might want to meet."

"You got them?" Sheriff Willis asked, his voice sounding surprised.

"I got them," Lawson replied, unable to keep the grin off his face. Yeah, maybe he shouldn't have been celebrating so soon, but any win was one he would welcome right now.

"Tell me what happened, exactly," Willis demanded. "I need to know what I'm dealing with here."

They had talked a few times about what they intended to do, but the guys had ended up making a few alterations at the last minute. Lawson stepped out of earshot and swiftly filled in the sheriff on the plan the guys had put together, with the broken-down vehicle on the side of the road as a lure. The guys who had turned up expecting a helpless woman were now cuffed to a metal pipe in a public restroom in the middle of nowhere.

Sheriff Willis let out a sigh.

"You bring them down to the station," he told him. "But like I said before, if you don't have anything we can pin on them right now, we're going to have to let them go. You hear me? I'm not intentionally bringing this kind of trouble into my town."

Lawson nodded, even though the sheriff couldn't see him. He got it. They couldn't just lock up these guys and throw away the key, no matter how much he would have liked to do just that. No, they had to go through the proper judicial process.

And if that meant Lawson needed to get a confession out of them before they could lock them up, so be it. He couldn't risk having to cut them loose, and allowing them to run back to Granger and tell him about their trap and that someone else was on their trail.

"I'll meet you at the station in an hour," he told the sheriff, and Sheriff Willis muttered his agreement, still clearly in the process of waking up.

Lawson turned his attention to the two men opposite him. Both of them were scowling, muttering curses at him with hatred in their eyes. If he was going to do this, he was going to have to get the information he needed from them quickly. He had about the length of the drive back to Blue Ridge to squeeze some of the truth out of them, and he hoped he'd scared them enough to get them to spill, one way or another.

He smirked, looking between them. "We've got a lot to talk about, boys," he told them, then went about undoing the cuffs from the pipe and dragging them to the truck waiting outside.

Chapter Thirteen

"We're here," Sarah breathed as she saw the lights of Warrior Peak come into view. This was what she needed right now—that sense of safety, that sense of calm. No matter how tempting it might have been to let the fear get the better of them, as long as they had made it to the lodge in one piece, everything was going to be okay. It had to be.

River turned the car off the main road and onto the connector road that led up to the lodge. As soon as she made the turn, she pulled over to the side and shut off the car lights; all the women held their breath as they waited to see what the car behind them was going to do. Sarah stared out the back window and, much to her surprise, the vehicle continued on up the road, without so much as slowing down.

Thank God. Maybe they had just been paranoid after all. She felt a little guilty for letting her nerves get the better of her, but she figured she was way better off being safe than sorry when it came to all of this. She didn't want to take any chances or make it easy for anyone to get close to them. Not when she knew what kind of danger was out there waiting for them. Much as she wanted to believe they'd already had their fair share of turmoil these last few months, she knew that life didn't work like that.

"Come on, let's get up to the lodge," Hannah said.

River turned on the car lights and they continued up to the main building. As soon as she parked in the gravel lot, River turned off the engine, and they all headed inside. Sarah could tell they were all lost in thought, wondering if they had been foolish in overthinking the possible threat, but it didn't matter. What mattered was that they were back now, and nothing was going to happen to them as long as they were here.

A few minutes later, as Hannah hung outside the front door with Sarah, Xavier's truck rushed up the driveway. Hannah breathed a sigh of relief, and she ran over to Xavier to give him a hug as soon as he stepped out. He wrapped his arms around her tightly and surveyed the area, making sure it was safe.

"You guys alright?" he asked as he led Hannah back toward Sarah.

"Yeah, we're fine," Sarah assured him. "We just got a little spooked by some guys at the bar, that's all. Thought they were following us, but whoever it was just continued down the road after we turned off. Guess they must be staying at one of the ranches nearby."

"Maybe seasonal workers," Xavier suggested as he pushed open the wooden door and led them inside.

"Maybe," Sarah agreed, chewing on her bottom lip. If she was being honest, there was only one thing on her mind right now and it was Lawson. She felt as though she would only be able to get her feet under her again when he was close to her.

"Where's Lawson?" she asked Xavier as she followed him. She tried to keep her voice neutral, but it came out a little more insistent than she had intended.

"He's surveilling at a rest stop about thirty miles away,"

Xavier replied. "Cade and Aaron were, too, but they're on their way back now."

"Why not him?" she asked, her stomach dropping. She knew it was silly, that Xavier never would have been so calm if he thought Lawson was in real danger, but she hated the thought of him not being here with everyone else. She was spooked and shaken, and she felt like his presence was the only thing that would ground her again.

"Hey," he murmured to her, seeming to sense how worried she was. "He's going to be okay. You know that, right?"

"I know that…"

"He's tough as nails," he reminded her. "And he can handle himself. Those guys who are going to run into him, they're the ones in danger. Not him."

Sarah thought back to what he said on the phone, that he wasn't in danger, but the men he was up against were about to be. She smiled slightly. She knew she should trust him on that. She knew he was good at what he did. She'd watched him and the others training before and knew he could handle himself.

And yet, she still wished he was here by her side more than anything right now. Not exactly the right attitude to have, and she knew it was selfish, given how important what he was taking on happened to be, but she couldn't help it.

They headed into the main greeting room and joined River and Bailey, who both looked tense. Xavier assured them that Cade and Aaron would be back soon, and she could see the relief on both their faces. She was happy for them, but she clutched her phone in her pocket, willing Lawson to call her so she could hear his voice and know he was fine.

Cade and Aaron arrived back a short time later, and the other women practically jumped on them in relief. Bailey scolded Aaron for not telling her about the mission they had been on, but Sarah could tell there was no real malice to it. Her face looked relieved and happy, not angry.

"Heard anything from Lawson?" Cade asked Xavier, his arm around River.

Xavier glanced over at Sarah, who shook her head.

"Just what Hannah relayed earlier," he replied. "He had a couple of them approaching the truck."

Cade's jaw tightened. He was trying to contain his concern, but Sarah was attuned to people's expressions and emotions because of her job. She could tell he was worried, and that had her feeling even more panicked. She tried to calm herself, digging her fingernails into her palm to ground herself, but it wasn't working.

All at once, her phone buzzed in her pocket, and she let out a yelp of surprise. She was so on edge, the noise had really startled her. She practically ripped her jacket pocket trying to get it out before the sound stopped, and she stared down at the screen. Lawson. Thank God.

"Is it him?" Xavier asked, and she nodded, lifting a hand to the group and stepping away so she could take the call in private.

"Lawson?" she answered, her voice a little shaky.

"Hey, Sarah," he replied. He sounded calm, and the soothing tone eased some of the tension in her. His voice was the best balm to her nerves right now.

"You guys okay?" he asked her. "You get back to the lodge?"

"Yeah, we're here now," she assured him. "The guys who were following us…well, they weren't following us. They carried on up the road after we pulled in. I guess we were just being jumpy, I'm sorry—"

"Hey, you've got nothing to be sorry about," he promised

her. “It’s better to be safe. The stakes are high right now and we’re all on edge. I’d much rather you were too cautious than anything else, you hear me?”

She smiled. He was so damn sweet. Even when she felt silly for making such a fuss, he was there to ground her, remind her that she was right to look out for herself.

“What about you?” she asked him. “When are you going to be back?”

He sighed, and suddenly his voice sounded tired. “It’s going to be a while,” he warned her. “Tell everyone not to wait up.”

“Really?” she asked, trying not to let the disappointment sound in her tone. She didn’t want to spook him or act entitled, but everyone else had their person right now. She didn’t know exactly where they stood, relationship-wise, but she knew she wanted him there with her.

“I have two of these bastards in custody,” he told her, and she could hear the proud grin in his words.

“You do?” she gasped.

“Yeah, the ruse worked and I nabbed a couple of them at the rest stop,” he explained. “Some of the sheriff’s men went up there to bring their car back down and they searched it. Found enough in there to keep them locked up for a while. Hopefully, as long as it takes to get to the answers we need.”

Sarah heard the pride in his voice, and he had every right to feel that way. One step closer to taking down these men was exactly what they needed right now, even if it meant he was going to be at the police station all night.

“You going to be okay?” he asked her gently.

“I’m going to be fine,” she promised him. “Everyone else is back and safe. I’m just anxious to see you. All that talk of missing women was just…surprising and unsettling.”

“I understand. It’s unsettling for all of us,” he replied.

"You just need to stay there and get some rest. Hopefully, this will all be over soon."

"I can tell how tired you are, Lawson. Are you sure you can't come back soon?" She hated the needy tinge in her voice but she still felt off and she was concerned about him.

"No," he said, sounding regretful. "I have a lot to deal with here at the police station. I don't want to leave until I know we have everything under control. Let the others know what's going on, okay?"

"Sure, I'll tell them," she agreed. "Just…don't push yourself too hard, okay? You take care of yourself."

"I will," he promised her softly. He lingered on the line for a moment, as though there was more he wanted to say. She knew how he felt.

All the stress from what had happened earlier in the night was still rushing around her head, and she knew she wasn't in a good state to be blurting out anything that might cross the line this early on in their budding relationship.

"I'll see you in the morning," he told her finally, and she bid him farewell, listening until he hung up the phone.

She stood there, phone pressed to her ear, recalling Lawson's voice, and holding it in her memory. She couldn't wait until she could see him again, give him a hug. To know for certain that he was as good as he claimed.

Sarah was ready for all of this to be over, to be able to move forward and figure out where they stood with each other. To be happy.

Together.

"What's going on?" Xavier asked her, snapping her back to reality.

"He's got a couple of the guys in lockup," she explained as she tucked her phone back into her pocket. "He said they got enough evidence from their vehicle to keep them locked up for a while. So that's good news, right?"

"That's great news," Xavier replied, breathing a sigh of relief. "I was worried that we were going to get them and they wouldn't have anything incriminating on them."

"You didn't have a plan in place?" Bailey asked, her eyes widening. She was a cop, so, of course, she was stressed at the thought of them not having something ready to go, but Sarah put a hand on her arm, trying to calm her down.

"It's okay," she reminded her. "They're in custody. That's all that matters."

"We had a plan," Cade offered. "We just had no way of knowing if whoever we caught would have anything illegal on them to keep them in jail."

"Come on, you guys need to get some rest," Aaron interrupted whatever else Bailey might have said, grabbing her hand. She glanced over at him, obviously still a little doubtful about the approach the guys had taken, but what mattered was that they had gotten the result they wanted.

Even if the guys should have been more careful in the way they went about it, two of Granger's men were in jail right now, and they would be able to get information out of them.

Or, at least, that was what she hoped.

Sarah headed back toward her cabin, counting out her footsteps, the stars still glittering in the night sky above. She knew she was going to have a hard time getting to sleep without Lawson back on the property, but she had to trust he knew what he was doing.

He was good at his job. Always had been. He could handle this.

Even if there was something nagging at the back of her

mind, telling her that this Granger person and his organization were worse than the men they had taken on before. And she hoped she never had to find just how right she might be.

Chapter Fourteen

Lawson lifted his head from the pillow with a groan. It felt like there was a drill going off behind his eyes, as his head was pounding painfully. He wasn't a young man anymore, and he couldn't get away with pulling all-nighters, like he had last night.

Well, he'd gotten an hour or two of sleep. By the time he had finished up at the police station for the night, leaving the sheriff and his deputies to get the two guys locked up and ready for interrogation, his head had been reeling from the chaos of the day behind him, and he hadn't been able to get any rest.

He needed to figure out how he could get the information out of the thugs about Granger and his operation. He had hoped they might have been Granger's sons, but no such luck. They were just a couple of lackeys, Jim Adams and Paul Donner, and they each had a rap sheet about half a mile long.

The sheriff's men had dug through their car and found enough drugs and unregistered guns to keep them locked up for a while longer, and the sheriff had promised Lawson that they weren't going to see sunlight unless it was to go to court.

Lawson was planning on going back down to the police station later in the day to speak to them himself. Since they were on that highway with the intention of grabbing a young woman, he knew they had to have some knowledge of Granger's operation, at least a location to deliver whomever they kidnapped. The question, though, was how loyal the two men were to their boss.

Would Lawson be able to rattle them enough to share information, or were they too scared of Granger and whatever he would have threatened them with to keep their mouths shut? He'd have to wait and see how it played out after he got there and started asking them questions.

He swung his legs out of bed and massaged his temples, knowing he was going to have to fill in Xavier and the others on what had happened the night before. He was sure they'd want to know details—the same ones he wanted to know himself that he obviously didn't have—but he could at least tell them the basics of what went down and provide the rest once he knew more.

The only way any of this operation was going to work for them, and to prepare his friends for whatever came next, would be to keep everyone updated on each step forward. No matter how small a detail was, it could end up leading toward the bigger picture.

Lawson was never big on postcase reports, and much rather preferred to be in the action and leave someone else see to the specifics, but he needed his team as strong and prepared as possible, and having all the necessary information to more forward would be the best way for that to happen.

He pulled the door open and was about to head downstairs to grab a coffee to wake himself up when he found Sarah standing in the hall, a couple of steaming mugs in her hands, and a smile on her face.

"Hey," she murmured, handing him a cup. "I figured you could use some caffeine after your late night."

He hesitated for a moment before taking the cup. He was sleep deprived and not really up to talking, and he knew she would have questions about what had gone down. He didn't want to worry her further.

"I can go, if you want," she told him, seeing his hesitation. "I know you must be exhausted."

"No, it's okay," he replied, and he gestured for her to step into his room. "Come on in."

He held the door for her, and glanced down at her face as she passed by him, noticing the dark rings around her eyes. Had she been up worrying about him all night? He hoped not. He didn't want her spending all her time concerned about what was going on with him when he knew he was well and truly capable of handling himself.

Plus, she had been so freaked out about the encounter with those guys last night at the bar. He knew she was right to be cautious, but he could tell that her previous experiences had left a stain on her psyche. She was hyperaware, jumping at every little noise. After everything she had been through, he couldn't say he blamed her.

She slipped into the seat at his desk and he planted himself down on the edge of the bed. Her eyes slipped to his hand, wrapped around the coffee cup, and she noticed a few grazes on it.

"Your hand..." she murmured, reaching out to touch it.

He winced and drew back, but shook his head quickly. "Nothing to worry about," he assured her. "They got it a lot worse than I did, trust me."

She smiled at him. "Good. I was so worried about you last night, I..."

She trailed off, and then shook her head. "I'm sorry, we

don't need to talk about that," she told him. "I'm just glad you're okay."

"Not to worry. I'm just tired," he reassured her. "It was a late night and I feel like I just closed my eyes."

She glanced around his room, and raised her eyebrows at the sight of a few plants sitting on a shelf next to the window.

"I didn't take you for much of a gardener," she remarked. "Especially with how you talk about Hannah's flowers."

"I'm not," he replied, chuckling. "Xavier just bullied me into having something in the rooms other than the bare minimum when we started this place."

"How do you mean?" she asked, cocking her head with interest.

"I just wanted this place to be simple," he explained. "I thought that would make things easy for the people who were staying here. The rooms were pretty bare back then, until Xavier said it looked like a prison, and we actually needed to make it more homey."

"And that's how he convinced you to put some plants up in your room?" she asked.

"Well, sort of," he said. "He had to show me a few studies about how improving our living space can have an impact on our mental health. And then I decided I could use some greenery around here."

"You'd make a great interior designer," she teased him. "Prison chic. I can see it being the next big thing."

"Maybe in another life." He laughed. Even though he was still exhausted, there was something about her company that sent a jolt of energy through his system. Well, that and the caffeine. That helped, too.

She got to her feet to admire his plants, and then, casually, sat down on the bed next to him. After their kiss, it felt like a far more pointed gesture than it might have before.

He shifted his leg so it was pressed against hers, his coffee cup resting on his thigh.

"So how are you doing? How's therapy going?" he asked her.

She sighed. "I'm doing okay, I guess. I'm still processing everything, I think," she responded. "I haven't been assigned a therapist yet, but should be soon. I'm worried I'm going to have trouble opening up to someone I don't know. Putting it all into the right words and having it make sense."

"Oh, yeah?" he prompted, frowning. "Why do you think that is?"

"Part of it, I think, is because of what I do. It's hard to be on the other side of the desk, you know? And also, with everything else happening around here, it's hard to know where to start," she admitted. "Especially when there's so much…other stuff going on now."

She glanced up at him, a small smile on her face.

He cocked an eyebrow. "Other stuff?" he asked her.

She nodded. "Other stuff," she repeated, as though daring him to ask her what.

"And what other stuff might that be?"

"Oh, well, that will be between my therapist and me," she replied playfully.

"You planning on talking about me in therapy?" he asked her.

She flashed him an impish smile, her cheeks flushing slightly. "Wouldn't you like to know," she retorted, shifting so she was pressed against his side.

This was comfortable, in a way Lawson wasn't sure he had felt in a long time. He decided then and there that he wasn't second-guessing this attraction he had to Sarah. He wasn't questioning if he was doing the wrong thing, for once in his damn life. He was just enjoying her company, the memory of their kiss and the new closeness it brought.

"I'd very much like to know," he replied, turning to face her and putting aside his coffee cup. "But I'm not going to pry," he murmured, reaching over to take her cup out of her hand, placing it next to his, then resting his hand on her cheek.

Sarah gazed up at him, leaning her head into his hand slightly, letting her eyes soften. She seemed to finally be able to relax after the chaos of what had happened the night before, and he was seriously glad for that. The last thing he wanted was for all of this to trigger more fear in her, to give her more trauma to deal with.

Slowly, he closed the distance between them, planting a soft kiss against her lips. She reached up to grasp his shoulder, her fingertips digging into his skin. God, she felt good. Even that kind of touch was enough to make the hairs on the back of his neck stand on end. He pulled back, brushing his nose against hers, and rested his forehead against hers.

"I can't wait until all of this stuff with Granger is behind us," he told her softly. "So I can put all my attention where it matters. On you."

She sank into him, letting a smile spread across her face. He loved seeing her like this, happy and relaxed, and just enjoying the moment with him. No matter what was going on outside his room, all he wanted right now was to lose himself to the feeling of the two of them together. Of her being in his arms and how perfect it felt.

"You have my attention right now," she murmured to him, her eyebrows raising, her teeth resting on her bottom lip.

He knew at once what she was suggesting. It had taken them a long time to get to this place, to acknowledge the way they felt about each other. To be in a place where they could finally act on their feelings. And damn, he wanted nothing more than to enjoy the stolen moment that they had been given right then.

He leaned close again, but this time, when their lips touched, he deepened the kiss. She parted her lips, allowing him to get closer, and he wrapped his arms around her, breathing in her scent. He felt the desire stirring inside him, and the need that he had tried to hold down for so long was rising up to take control.

And, in the soft morning light pouring through the window behind them, he knew he was finally ready. They were both finally ready.

He sank down into the bed with her, grinning into the kiss.

Chapter Fifteen

Sarah gazed up at the ceiling, a dizzying smile on her face. She could still feel the pleasure tingling through every inch of her body as she lay beneath the covers in Lawson's bed.

That had been…*whoa.* So much better than her fantasies of them together. Her head was still spinning from their intense connection—it was more than she could ever have expected. They had been dancing around their feelings for each other for so long, she had been starting to think it would never happen.

From the moment their lips had touched, she felt herself give in to him, her body accepting this closeness for the first time. No, more than accepting it, she *needed* it, craved it from some place deep inside her.

He glanced over at her as he buttoned up his shirt, flashing her a sexy grin.

"You good?" he asked her.

"Better than good," she replied with a sigh, flipping over to face him. "You sure you can't stay a little longer?"

"I would love to, trust me," he admitted, pulling a face, and planted himself down on the bed next to her. He took her hand and drew it to his lips, placing a kiss against it softly. If she hadn't already been lying down, she would have swooned on the spot.

"But I have to go into town and talk to the sheriff about what we're going to do next with those assholes he's got in jail." He sighed, running a hand through his hair.

She propped herself up in the bed and shrugged. "How about I come with you?" she suggested. "I have some groceries to pick up in town and Hannah asked me to grab a few items for the kitchen, too. I was going to ask one of the guys to go with me, but I'd much rather go with you. If I wouldn't be in the way, that is?"

He paused for a moment, then smiled and nodded. "You know what, I'd love that," he replied.

"I'll get dressed," she said coyly, flashing him a playful little grin. As much as she knew she would have enjoyed lounging around naked with him, they had stuff to take care of, and she wasn't going to be the one to hold him up.

"While you're doing that, I'm going to call Xavier really quick and tell him we're running to town and that I'll fill them in on everything when we get back." He gave her a quick kiss on the forehead, then stepped in the hall to make the call.

When she was dressed, they walked down to his truck. He looped his little finger around hers, holding on gently, like he was making sure she didn't drift away. She could hardly keep the grin off her face. She knew the other women would have a ton of questions for her if they saw the two of them together, but honestly, right now, she was finding it hard to mind much. Maybe she wanted people to see them like this, just to make sure it was real.

He offered her a hand to help her into the truck, and she rolled down the window as they pulled away. It was another beautiful day, and the sunshine filled the cab. Sarah snuck a look at him out of the corner of her eye, and felt her chest flutter slightly again. It felt so damn good to be with him like this.

"It's gorgeous today," she remarked, holding her hand out of the window and swimming it through the cool air.

"It really is," he replied, his eyes lingering on her for a second longer than necessary.

She laughed, her cheeks flushing slightly. It was like he could hardly keep his eyes on the road, the sight of her too exciting to deny. As he drove, he reached over to rest a hand on the inside of her thigh. His touch was strong and grounding, and she couldn't stop stealing glances at his hand. It was so new, but at the same time, his presence was so familiar, as though this was where the two of them had always belonged.

For a moment, even though she knew it wasn't going to last long, she felt as though the weight of everything that was going on around them was lifting from her mind and she could finally relax. Of course, she knew it wasn't that easy, but she was happy, and with Lawson, and she just wanted to take a moment to enjoy it.

He pulled the truck to a halt in the town square, and he offered her a hand to help her out. He dropped a kiss on her cheek before he looked over toward the jail.

"You going to be alright?" he asked her, concerned.

"I'm just going to the store." She laughed. "I'm going to be fine."

"You better be," he warned her playfully, and she kissed him again. She couldn't get enough of him right now. "I'll see you in a bit."

She watched him walk toward the station, then turned and headed in the direction of the store. As she made her way across the street, her attention was drawn to the bar she and her friends had been to last night. She paused when she reached the sidewalk. Maybe she could just pop in for a minute and ask about those guys from last night? See if they were regulars or passing through. Help put her mind at ease.

Even though there was a Closed sign in the window, she knocked on the door, and a moment later, an older woman's face appeared through the glass before she opened the door to greet her.

"Everything alright?" she asked.

"Sorry to bother you," Sarah blurted out. "I just… I wanted to ask you about a couple of guys who were in here last night?"

"The ones who ordered those drinks for you and your friends, you mean?" she asked, nodding knowingly.

"You've got a good memory. Yeah, those guys," Sarah replied. "Have you seen them around before?"

"I have," she responded. "They pass through here on their way to work a few times a year. Not exactly the most clean-cut guys you'll ever meet, but they're harmless enough."

"Right," Sarah said, breathing a sigh of relief. "Sorry to bother you. Thanks."

"Sure," the woman replied, and she closed the door again and set about taking care of whatever she had been doing before Sarah had interrupted her.

Sarah closed her eyes for a moment and inhaled deeply. See? There was nothing for her to worry about—those guys had just been trying their luck, hitting up her and her friends in the hopes they might turn out to be single. She didn't have to read anything else into it.

She hooked her bag over her shoulder and headed off toward the store, feeling a little lighter. She knew that last night had just been her fear and anxiety getting the better of her, and she was a little embarrassed about it. Even though Lawson had told her there was no problem with her playing it safe, she couldn't help but wonder if he was secretly rolling his eyes at her behind her back.

No, he would never have done that, and she knew it. He just wasn't that kind of guy. What you saw was what you got with him. It was one of the reasons she liked him so much.

"Sarah?"

She startled, then grinned when she saw Lawson coming toward her, then cocked her head, a little confused.

"I thought you were interviewing those guys today?"

"I was supposed to, but Sheriff Willis is out right now. I guess I should have called first," he replied. "You need a hand with that grocery shopping?"

"Oh, I could always use a big strong man to help carry the bags." She laughed, handing him the reusable ones she had brought with her. "Here, you take these."

They walked to the grocery store, and she hummed along to the tinny music playing over the speakers as they picked out dinner together. It felt almost surreal, doing something as mundane as this with him, but in a good way. She'd love to repeat it as often as she got the chance. Maybe that was a little selfish, but hell, who could blame her? She loved having him all to herself.

As they checked out, she felt eyes on her and looked over to see Lawson watching her. She glanced up at him with a smile and he winked back, causing her to blush. They made small talk while the cashier continued to ring up their groceries and it felt like the most natural thing in the world. They seemed to share an easy rhythm between them and Sarah had to reach out and touch his hand just to make sure she wasn't dreaming. He squeezed her hand back, and then they gathered the bags and headed back to the truck to load them up.

"I think this is going to be enough to keep us going all summer." He laughed.

She shrugged. "Hey, not all of it is for me. Plus, I like to think ahead," she replied as they climbed back into the truck. But, before they could drive off, Lawson got a text on his phone. He looked down at it and grimaced slightly.

"What is it?" she asked.

"The sheriff," he replied. "He says I should head over there now. They're ready for me." He glanced over at her. "You want me to drive you back up to the lodge?" he asked. "I can come back down afterward, it's no trouble…"

"Don't be silly," she answered, shaking her head. "You don't need to go all the way up there and back again. You'll spend two hours just driving. It's daytime and I'm perfectly capable of driving myself. How long do you think you'll be?"

"A few hours, at least."

"Text me when you're done," she suggested. "And I'll come pick you up."

"You don't have to—"

"I know I don't," she replied softly, reaching over to touch his arm lightly. "I want to, Lawson. I want to help."

"Okay, well, if you're sure," he said as he handed Sarah his keys.

"I'll go up and drop off the groceries and check in with everyone, then I'll come back down and grab myself a coffee while I wait," she suggested. "I don't have any appointments today and I could use the change of scenery."

"You going to be alright on your own?"

"Of course, I will," she replied. "I might have been a little out of sorts last night, but I can handle myself. You don't have to worry about me."

A weight seemed to ease from his shoulders when she

said that, and she was so glad to see him give in and stop worrying about her for a change. It wasn't that she hadn't given him reason to be concerned over these last few weeks, but the last thing she wanted was for him to neglect other things he needed to focus on to hover around her.

There was only one main road up the mountain to the lodge and she knew it like the back of her hand. Plus, it was the middle of the day, so she knew there'd be no trouble on the road right now. The men Lawson and the others were after, including the two locked up at the police station, skulked around in the dark of night. No way would they try something in daylight, on a well-traveled road where anyone could drive by and see. Those kind of men preferred the shadows to keep them safe.

Sarah sat and watched as Lawson crossed the street to the police station. He turned to wave at her before he went inside, and she waved back and then put the truck in gear and pulled out on to the road. A truck full of groceries, a sky full of sunshine and a sweet man waiting for her to come pick him up. Did it get any better than that?

Chapter Sixteen

Lawson entered the police station, where Sheriff Willis was waiting for him, arms crossed, a terse expression on his face.

"Finally, you're here," he muttered. "Kept me waiting long enough."

Lawson stopped in his tracks. "You weren't around when I first came by," Lawson pointed out, cocking an eyebrow at the sheriff. If there was one thing he had never credited the sheriff with, it was a short temper.

Sheriff Willis rubbed a hand over his face. There were dark rings beneath his eyes, and Lawson couldn't help but feel a little sorry for him. Clearly, it had been a long-ass night, dealing with those two prisoners in lockup, and it looked as though it was taking its toll.

"You good?" Lawson asked him.

The sheriff nodded. "Sorry. Just wish they weren't in my station, that's all," he replied, nodding in the direction of the cells that held the two prisoners.

"They been giving you trouble?"

"They've been talking a big game," Sheriff Willis muttered, sighing. "Giving my officers plenty to think about. Seems like Granger taught them to be as difficult as possible while they were under lock and key. Probably thought it would get them released sooner that way."

"Sorry you had to be involved in this. Thanks for dealing with them," Lawson replied grimly. He could only imagine what kind of trash talk the thugs had been saying to the police officers who worked here. All the threats and taunts they were probably maliciously spewing to get a reaction, or cause the officers to drop their guards so they could get the upper hand.

"I understand why they're here. I just hope this can get wrapped up quickly. They're both causing such a ruckus, none of my officers are comfortable being around them," the sheriff remarked as he went to grab the keys from behind the counter. "When you're done, we'll get them transferred over to the FBI and it can become their headache. Our small town isn't set up to handle something of this magnitude."

Lawson couldn't help but feel bad for the man, especially with all the danger that had surrounded the lodge over the past couple of years. Normally, Blue Ridge was a quiet, peaceful town that didn't see much action in terms of criminal activity. There had been a lot the sheriff had to step in and deal with concerning the lodge that no one had expected or been prepared for. None of them at Warrior Peak had any idea of the constant danger they would face.

They were all ready for it to be over and done with, so they could get back to their normal day-to-day without having threats and danger constantly hanging over the heads. They were all due a break.

"Have you already contacted the FBI?" Lawson asked as they made their way to the interrogation rooms. He knew there was a chance the FBI would step in immediately, but he was hoping he'd at least be able to take a quick stab at the suspects before they were taken into FBI custody.

"I did," Sheriff Willis replied. "I filled them in on everything you told me and sent what information I had over to them. They've got some agents on the way, said they'd probably be here tomorrow."

"So what you're saying is I've got one shot to talk to them both, see what I can find out before they're gone," Lawson confirmed, and the sheriff nodded with a grim smile.

"Sorry I couldn't give you more time. I just want them out of here. All this trafficking stuff is too dangerous for our small-town police station." Sheriff Willis gestured down the hallway. "Donner's in the first interrogation room," he told him. "You ready to get started?"

"Yep, let's do this," Lawson replied, steeling himself for what lay ahead.

Lawson had looked over Paul Donner's rap sheet the previous night while he'd been at the station, and it was pretty impressive, he had to admit. Impressive in a way that he was surprised Donner had been able to set foot outside a prison at all. Assault, drug charges, illegal possession of a weapon, attempted murder...the list went on. Obviously, Granger had the right kind of connections to keep his guys from doing hard time.

Sheriff Willis unlocked the door, and Lawson led the way inside. Donner was cuffed to the table, and he shook his chains demonstratively as soon as Lawson stepped inside.

"Let me out of these," he snarled, and Lawson ignored him. The man was going to throw as much nonsense as he could at them to avoid dealing with the real questions at hand, and it was up to Lawson to keep his cool. He'd handled plenty of people like Donner over the years, and if the man thought he was going to get under his skin, he didn't stand a chance.

Lawson sat down opposite the perp, while the sheriff stood behind Lawson, hands clasped before him, like a security guard.

"I don't know what I'm doing here," Donner snapped. "This is false arrest!"

"Really, Mr. Donner?" Lawson asked. "Because I've had a look at your file. And with the stuff they found in your car alone, you'd go down for many years. Not to mention the attempted kidnapping charge."

"What kidnapping?" the man retorted. "I didn't kidnap anyone." He leaned back in his seat smugly, locking eyes with Lawson. "I think you should be the one on this side of the table," he remarked. "You're the one who assaulted us. When we hadn't done anything wrong. We were just going to use the bathroom."

Lawson steadily held the other man's gaze and raised an eyebrow at his comments. Donner could try to spin the arrest any way he wanted, but Lawson wasn't stupid. He knew exactly what the thug and his buddy were out there to do. And it certainly wasn't to use the facilities.

Sheriff Willis snorted with amusement, and Donner's eyes darkened.

Lawson calmly clasped his hands in front of him on the table. "What can you tell us about Victor Granger and his operation?" he began. "If you share what you know, we can see about cutting you a deal, like Mr. Adams."

For the briefest moment, Lawson could see the doubt in the other man's eyes, as he wondered if what Lawson had said was true. Lawson stared back at him, poker face in place, keeping up the act, but then Donner's lip curled into a sneer.

"Yeah, no way has he said anything about anything," he replied. "Nice try, man. You have any clue what Victor does to snitches? Worse than anything you could think of."

"So, fill us in. Tell us what we need to know," Lawson said. "Give us his location. Tell us about his operation. We won't let on that you gave anything away. It's your best chance for a lighter sentence. If you show some kind of co-operation."

Donner barked out a harsh laugh, shaking his head. "You people… This little backwoods town has no clue the nightmare he'll rain down on you all. You'll never be able to sleep again, wondering when he's coming for you, or what he'll do to you and anyone you care about."

Lawson felt his muscles tense at Donner's words, and he saw the sheriff shifting uncomfortably from the corner of his eye. Sheriff Willis was already unsettled enough about these two men being in his station, and he didn't need to hear this. It would only make his apprehension about the whole affair worse.

Watching Donner across the table and seeing the fear flickering in his eyes at what his boss might do to him had Lawson wondering exactly what kind of horrors Granger had drilled into his men's heads about the consequences of snitching if they were caught. He almost didn't want to know.

Suddenly, Donner's eyes went flat and darkened, his gaze locked on Lawson with what looked like madness.

"You go after Victor, it'll be the last mistake you ever make," he warned Lawson, his eyes burning. "You and everyone you know. You have no idea how dangerous he is."

"Why don't you tell us, then? Help us and yourself."

"You don't have a damn clue." He laughed again, the sound bouncing off the walls around them. "I'm going to enjoy seeing you find out."

Lawson could see why the sheriff had looked so exhausted when he had arrived today. All the crap Donner was spouting off, and he assumed Jim Adams would be the same.

"You're going to get yourselves killed and you're going to deserve it," he continued, an evil grin spreading over his face. "I wish I could be there when it happens. You'll find out soon enough who you're dealing with."

"We're not getting anything out of him. Come on, Lawson, let's go," Sheriff Willis muttered behind him.

Lawson rose to his feet and tried not to react to the sheriff saying his name in front of this thug.

A thoughtful look crossed Donner's face, then he grinned. "Lawson, huh?" he remarked. "Not a common name. Especially around these parts. You think he won't be able to find you? You're a walking dead man, Lawson."

Lawson glared back at him, trying not to let the fear that gripped his chest take hold.

Normally, he'd let this kind of threat bounce off, but now? Now, he had something to lose. All he could think of was Sarah and all she'd been through recently. Then his thoughts quickly shifted to his sister and the others at the lodge. The thought of Granger and his men coming after any of them had a chill racing down Lawson's spine. He had to admit to himself it spooked the hell out of him and he couldn't even try to deny it.

They stepped out of the interrogation room, Lawson shutting the door behind them, and the sheriff grimaced and rubbed a hand down his face.

"I'm sorry for dropping your name back there. Rookie mistake," he apologized. "I'm tired. I wasn't thinking."

"It's okay," Lawson replied, though his gut was churning. "They would have found out who I was one way or another, anyway."

Sheriff Willis lowered his voice and looked over his shoulder, like someone might be eavesdropping on their conversation. "These guys have me rattled," he admitted.

"I've had some rough types in here before, don't get me wrong, but this…the way they're coming at us, it's just different. Like they know they've got the devil on their side, and they'll do anything they can to turn him loose on us."

"I get it. Don't let them get to you," Lawson warned him. "That's what they want. Until they give us reason to think otherwise, they're all bark."

The sheriff nodded, but there was still a wariness to his expression, as though he didn't entirely believe Lawson's claim. Lawson had to hope it was just because the older man was exhausted, not because he was actually letting these guys get to him.

"Where's Adams?" he asked, steeling himself for round two. His rap sheet hadn't been as impressive as Donner's, but he still had plenty on it to keep him locked up.

The sheriff nodded to the cells lining the end of the corridor.

"Down there," he replied. Lawson gritted his teeth. He silently swore to himself that no matter what this guy threw at him, he would be able to deal with it. These weren't the worst of the people they'd have to handle if they were going to take down Granger, and Lawson wasn't going to let these thugs throw him off his game.

The moment they reached Jim Adams's cell, the man was on his feet, pressed against the bars.

"Where's Paul?" he demanded.

"None of your business," Lawson replied. Adams gripped the bars, his hands holding on so tightly his knuckles looked nearly white.

"Tell me what you've done with him," he continued, practically spitting out the words.

"You don't trust him?" Lawson asked. "You think he

might have spilled something? Or sold you out for a plea deal?"

Unlike his buddy, Adams didn't even seem to consider that as a possibility for a moment. He snorted with amusement.

"You think that he would sell out Granger like that? For a speck on the map like you?" he demanded, jabbing his finger through the bars at Lawson. Lawson took a step back, not wanting this creep to lay a hand on him.

"You know what he's going to do with you the moment he finds out about this?" he continued, his voice rising with each word out of his mouth. "He's going to wipe you off the face of the earth. There's going to be nothing of you left! Do you understand that? There's nothing you can do to stop it! He's coming for you right now!"

Adams kept babbling, barely pausing to take a breath. Spittle was flying from his mouth as he spoke, and the cell bars rattled as he shook them. He was getting more agitated and animated over the words he threw at them. The churning in Lawson's gut intensified as he watched the man become more unhinged.

Lawson was starting to get a clearer picture of the hold Granger had on his men. Apparently, it bordered on the extreme, and Lawson in no way wanted to know what the man had done to his crew to have this Adams go off the rails like this. If all of the men in Granger's operation held this kind of loyalty, Lawson and his team were definitely going to be in for the fight of their lives when it came time to face him and his gang of thugs.

"And you're going to end up dead. You and everyone you care about." Adams spat at them, then fell back on the bench and started cackling gleefully.

Lawson's heart dropped. *Sarah.* Once again, she was the

first person he thought of when Adams said that. He would never forgive himself if something bad happened to her as a result of them going after Granger and his crew. He could still remember the terror he'd seen in her eyes from the fire and its aftermath, when Bailey and Aaron's past caught up with them at the lodge all those months ago. The thought of her being dragged into more danger because of her connection to Lawson made him feel sick.

Adams seemed to realize he'd landed a blow that actually hurt. His eyes drilled in to Lawson's, total certainty on his face, as though there wasn't a doubt in his mind that he was telling the truth.

"Tick tock. It's only a matter of time now," Adams said, tapping a watch that wasn't there.

Lawson gritted his teeth. He had told the sheriff not to let these guys get to him, but Lawson wasn't sure he could take his own advice.

Chapter Seventeen

Sarah lifted the decaf coffee to her lips and took a sip, enjoying the last of the late afternoon sunshine as the day began to shift into evening.

She had been back to the lodge, dropped off the groceries, checked in with Hannah and Xavier, and returned a few emails before she made the hour-long drive back into town to pick up Lawson from the police station. She sent him a text when she arrived, telling him to meet her at the corner café across the street when he was done. He hadn't responded so she had no idea how long he would be, but that was just fine by her. She was happy to relax, sip on her coffee and nibble at the carrot cake she had ordered. It wasn't often she got a chance to come to town and people-watch like this, but there was something really fun about observing the townsfolk going about their business.

Her interest in people, after all, had been what had gotten her into her line of work in the first place. She was always curious about what was going on in people's lives and in their minds, and how she could help them deal with their problems and emotions. She found the human brain so fascinating.

As she watched couples chatting and kids running around, she smiled. It was hard to believe that a town like this could have a possible sex-trafficking problem, though she doubted anyone she was currently observing here would know a thing about it.

And she hoped it stayed that way. Now that Lawson had gotten those two guys into custody, it was surely only a matter of time before they got the information they needed to take down Granger and shut down his operation.

Finally, as she finished up her coffee, she spotted Lawson coming out of the police station across the street. Even from here, she could tell he had a grim expression on his handsome face. He must not have gotten the information he needed, she thought. She tossed her trash and walked out to meet him.

"How did it go?" she asked him softly, reaching for his hand and giving him his keys back.

He frowned. "Not as well as I'd hoped," he admitted. He switched the keys to his other hand, then entwined his fingers with hers.

"You didn't get much out of them?"

"We didn't get anything out of them," he replied, shaking his head. "But I expected that. It was… They seemed like they were enjoying themselves and weren't worried at all about giving anything away."

"What do you mean?" she asked, frowning. That didn't make any sense to her. Why would they have enjoyed being interrogated? They had to know that the business they were involved with was seriously dangerous, and they would be facing years, maybe even decades, in prison if the truth of everything they had done came out.

"Instead of answering questions they were taunting the officers, making them uncomfortable, and spewing threats. Just trying to get a rise out of everyone," he admitted, as they walked hand in hand toward the truck, which was parked in the town square. "One thing they both kept saying was that Granger was going to come after us. Going to…"

He trailed off, shaking his head as he reached the truck and unlocked the door, like he had all at once decided that she didn't need to hear the rest. A shiver ran down her spine. She didn't want him keeping things from her, but judging by the look on his face, she had to trust that she was better off not knowing.

"It's okay," she told him softly. "You did your best, right? And what matters is that you have them locked up. They aren't out there trying to take more young women. That has to count for something."

"You're right," he acknowledged, but the furrow between his eyebrows told a different story. She knew that he wanted to get to the bottom of it all. She wished she could help in some way. But she had learned the hard way that nothing came that easy—

All at once, the quiet of the town square was shattered by a noise. A popping sound. Then another.

At first, Sarah thought it was a car backfiring. But, as Lawson spun around to step in front of her, she realized what it actually was.

Gunshots. Someone was shooting.

"Get in the truck and get your head down!" Lawson ordered her as he yanked open the driver's-side door and grabbed something from underneath the seat. She stood there for a moment, frozen, unable to move.

"Sarah, now!" he yelled at her, and it snapped her out of her fugue state. She dived into the truck, ducking down on the floorboard, and wrapped her arms around her knees as her heart pounded in her chest. Her mind was racing. What the hell was going on out there? Why was someone shooting? It had been so peaceful, so safe, and now…it was shattered by the sound of gunfire.

She jolted as a bullet hit the side of the truck, a dent appearing in the door just a few inches from her. Her eyes widened, panic flooding her system.

Another bullet hit the metal, and another, the dents pushing inward, like the side of the truck was about to buckle in on itself. Was Lawson okay? If the bullets were hitting the truck, then they weren't hitting him, right?

She heard another gunshot, this time sounding closer, and wrapped her arms around her head, trying to block out the noise. She was shaking and started to whimper, but could hardly pay attention. Loud. It was all so loud and terrifying. She wanted to see what was going on but was scared to move. She couldn't believe this was happening right now. And Lawson… Where was he?

Suddenly there was silence. It was almost deafening—it had gotten so quiet so fast. Sarah's heart thudded in her chest and she held her breath, praying that Lawson was going to call her name. She needed to know he was okay. If something had happened to him, she didn't know what she would do…

And then, all at once, the door next to her opened. She jerked back and screamed. But instead of some would-be attacker, Lawson stood there, staring down at her with fury in his eyes.

"You okay?" he asked urgently.

She pulled her arms away from her head and looked up at him slowly, and then nodded. "I think so," she breathed. Her mouth was dry and her body felt numb. She'd been crumpled up on the floorboard and she wasn't sure she could get her limbs to cooperate. She didn't think she'd been hit, though there had been a lot of bullets pinging off the truck's frame. She couldn't be sure until her body was completely functioning again.

And the same couldn't be said for Lawson.

Her eyes widened when she saw a red stain on his right side. She reached out to grab his shirt and pulled it up, revealing a bloody gash on his skin.

"What happened?" she exclaimed, terror flashing in her eyes. She tried to squirm her way off the floorboard.

"It's fine, just a graze," he assured her, gently brushing her hand away. As he shifted, she noticed that he had a gun in his other hand. So the shots she'd heard from nearby had been from him.

"Just a graze?" she exclaimed. "You're bleeding!"

"I'll be fine," he promised her. "Can you step out of the truck? I want to get a look at you."

With Lawson's hand under her arm, and Sarah pushing up on the seat, she managed to get herself up and stepped out of the truck.

First thing she noticed was that the square was empty—everyone who had been here before must have scattered when the gunfire started. She knew this incident would change the fabric of the town entirely.

She craned her head around as Lawson looked her over and her heart dropped when she saw someone sprawled, not moving, on the ground next to the police station.

Lawson saw her staring, and shifted so that he was blocking her view.

"Hey, you don't need to see that," he told her gently.

"Who is that?" she demanded, voice trembling. "The sheriff?"

"No, the sheriff's okay."

"Well, who is that? What happened?" she asked again.

"I don't know exactly yet," he admitted with a sigh. "But

Donner and Adams were both rushing out of the station firing, so I'd guess somehow they managed to get weapons off a couple officers inside and made a run for it. The sheriff and his guys are not used to dealing with men like these."

"They both had guns?" she gasped. "And they—they were shooting at you?"

"Yeah, trying to make good on their threats, I suppose," he replied as he gazed down at her. She could feel the tension radiating off him, and she knew he must be unnerved by what happened, though he was doing everything he could not to let her see it.

"So the dead guy is one of them?"

He gestured behind him, toward the unmoving body on the sidewalk. "Jim Adams."

"Oh," she replied. A bad guy was dead. And Lawson, if she was guessing right, had been the one to kill him. The thought made her stomach twist into knots. He'd done what he'd had to do, of course, but she had never imagined she would see something like that, and definitely not here in Blue Ridge.

"And what about the other one?" she asked.

"Donner made a break for it," he admitted.

Her eyes widened. They hadn't recaptured him. The other man was gone. Sarah wrapped her arms around her middle. The thought of that man running back to Granger and then him setting his sights on this town… The danger around them had just multiplied tenfold.

A few officers emerged from the station to deal with the mess that had been left outside their building and to take care of Jim Adams's body. The sun was fading now, bringing a dark night. A cold chill ran through Sarah's body, though she knew it was nothing to do with the weather.

"They said they were going to come after you," she muttered.

Lawson nodded. "They did," he replied.

She could tell by his posture that he wished he hadn't told her that. But that didn't matter now. She already knew they'd all be in danger when the guys first set out to find the men kidnapping women on the mountain road.

"So, what now?" she asked as they continued to glance around the damaged town square.

"I've got to go back over and give a statement and check in with the sheriff," Lawson told Sarah. "Do you want to come with me, or go back and wait inside the café?"

Sarah shivered again and shook her head. No way was she staying here by herself, not after what just happened. "I'll come with you," she said quickly and latched on to his hand.

Lawson nodded and wrapped his arm around her as they made their way across the square and back into the police station, meeting Sheriff Willis at the door. He left Sarah in the waiting area and followed the angry sheriff back to the interrogation room.

After what felt like forever, Lawson reemerged looking more haggard and holding his side like he was in pain.

He walked right up to Sarah and drew her into his arms, then kissed her forehead.

"Come on, we need to get you back to the lodge," he told her. She didn't speak as he steered her gently back toward the truck. Gun smoke still lingered in the air, the scent of it cloying in her nostrils. She wanted to forget this had ever happened, but she knew it wouldn't be that easy. Especially with Lawson being hurt.

"You should have had someone look at your wound while you were in there," she gently chided.

He shook his head, opened the passenger door, and helped

her inside. After sliding into the driver's seat, he palmed the wheel and glanced over at her. He must have noticed her expression and knew how much the situation was getting to her.

"It's going to be okay, Sarah," Lawson told her, putting a hand on hers and giving it a tight squeeze.

And, as much as she wanted to believe him, she had no idea if she actually could. Not with one of those men on the loose, and not when he was likely running back to his boss to tell him all about them.

Chapter Eighteen

Lawson gently pressed the cloth against Sarah's arm as she perched on the edge of his bed. She was staring off into space like she had no idea at all where she was.

The lodge was quiet except for the raised voices Lawson could hear drifting up from downstairs. He knew the guys were arguing about what had happened in town and what the best course of action would be now that Adams had escaped.

As soon as Lawson and Sarah had arrived back at the lodge, he'd asked her to wait for him in his room while he talked to the guys. After she went upstairs, he had filled Cade, Xavier and Aaron in on everything that had happened since the previous night. The rest stop bust, Adams's and Donner's interrogations, their escape, and Adams's death by Lawson's hand.

The guys were just as concerned about Donner's words as Lawson was. Even though the man only had Lawson's first name, if someone had the right resources it wouldn't take them long to find out his last name, as well as information about Warrior Peak and the others there. Victor Granger could easily be that someone.

Lawson left the guys discussing plans while he went to check on Sarah. His mind kept turning to her while they were talking and he needed to reassure himself that she was truly okay.

"You should be down there with them," she mumbled.

He lifted his gaze to meet hers. There was a long, thin cut on the side of her arm from where she had dived into the truck to take cover. Neither of them had noticed until she mentioned the sting on the drive back, and he was cleaning it up before he walked her back to her cabin to get some rest.

"They can deal with it for now," he replied, though he knew she was right. These guys relied on him to lead their team, and he needed to be involved in whatever plans they were making next, so he did need to get downstairs and meet with them soon.

But Sarah had been trembling like a leaf when they had arrived back at the lodge, and he knew he needed to take care of her first. He couldn't even imagine how terrified she had been when she had heard those gunshots going off in town. He was used to this, to some extent, between the military and his stint in the CIA, even if Blue Ridge town square had been the very last place he had imagined having to fight off attackers.

But her? She wasn't used to this. She needed help. The adrenaline would still be coursing through her system right now, and he couldn't leave her alone.

He smoothed the cloth over her arm, and she twisted it around to look at the angry red mark on the back of her forearm.

"It's not that bad," she told him.

"I hate that you got hurt at all," he muttered. At least she hadn't been shot. His side had been grazed, but he could barely feel it. He would likely start to feel that all-too-familiar sting soon, but he didn't care about that at all when she was so scared and needed him to comfort her.

"What about you?" she asked, nodding to his wound.

He glanced down at the stain of blood on his shirt and shrugged. "It's fine," he replied. "I doubt it even needs stitches."

"Let me have a look, at least," she insisted, peeling up his shirt and wincing when she saw his side.

"That looks bad," she murmured, and he grabbed a bandage from the first aid kit and slapped it on to appease her. He didn't want her worrying about him. She needed to focus on herself and her own mental health. He could tell on the drive back to the lodge that she was starting to withdraw into herself from stress and fear. He wanted to help her calm down and he hoped that reassuring her that he was alright would help with that.

"It'll heal in no time," he assured her. "I've had plenty worse, trust me."

She managed a small smile. "That doesn't make me feel better," she said, and he kneeled before her, hands on her legs.

"What would make you feel better?" he asked her.

She took a deep breath. "I want you to be honest with me," she replied. "What happens now that one of them has gotten away?"

He sighed. He knew he owed her the truth, after what she had just been through, but he wasn't sure she would be able to handle it. She looked down at him, kneeling in front of her, her eyes full of certainty. She deserved to know what came next, and he believed she was strong enough to take it in stride.

"It means that Donner will be heading back to Granger," he explained. "And that we don't have the element of surprise on our side anymore. Or time. He'll do his research on us, find out who we are and where we are. Then he's going to make a move. It'll be fast. Now that he knows what went down and that we're trying to disrupt his operations."

She nodded, letting out a shaky breath.

"That's pretty much what I thought," she said. "What—what are we going to do?"

"I don't know yet," he admitted. "I need to talk with the guys, and fill Lainey in on what happened earlier."

In the chaos of everything that had been going on, he had almost forgotten about Lainey, which he felt guilty about now. What if they knew where she was and went after her? He didn't think that was possible, since no one knew she had been there. But if Granger really had the connections all over the place like Lainey claimed he did, she could be in more trouble than she realized.

"Why don't you give her a call to tell her what's happening?" Sarah suggested.

"Good idea," he agreed, and he pulled out his phone and dialed Lainey's number, resting his arm on the bed next to Sarah as he did so. She rubbed his shoulders gently, as though she could sense how tense he was.

No answer. He ended the call and tried again…and again, and again. But nothing. His jaw tensed. He didn't like this, not one bit. Especially not after the events of the day.

He put his phone away, and Sarah slipped her arms around him, searching his eyes. For what, he wasn't sure, but decided not to ask. He knew she was concerned for him, just as he was for her.

"She's probably fine," she assured him. "Maybe she's in the shower or stepped out for a minute or something. I bet she'll call you as soon as she sees she missed your call."

"I hope so," he said, though he wasn't sure he entirely believed it.

She leaned her head against his for a moment, and he

closed his eyes. He just wanted this to be over. Maybe he never should have gotten involved with this in the first place, but he knew there was no way he could let Lainey face this on her own. She was his friend, after all, and he stood by his friends, no matter how hard it might be, or what dangerous situations they needed help with.

"I've got this…feeling," she murmured, her voice tinged with worry. "Like something bad's going to happen."

He opened his eyes and pulled back, gathering her in his arms.

"It's going to be fine," he promised her with as much certainty as he could muster. "Try not to worry, I'll do everything in my power to protect you."

"I know. I trust you."

He planted a kiss on her lips, sealing his promise. He didn't care what happened next, he didn't care what kind of danger he had to face to keep her safe—he would do it.

"Come on, let's get you back to your cabin. I'll tell the guys we'll meet in the morning. I think we could all use a good night's rest." He held on to her hand as they walked down the stairs and out of the lodge.

When they got to her door, he gave her one more kiss and waited until she was inside before heading back to the lodge to tell the guys they'd meet tomorrow.

He wasn't sure what would come next, but he did know they all needed to be alert and ready.

"So let me get this straight. You were almost shot dead in the town square?" Hannah asked Lawson, raising her eyebrows at him in horror.

"He was never going to get me from that angle," he protested. "And besides, I had a gun. I could protect myself."

The air was tense this morning while all eight of them

gathered in the main greeting area of the lodge and went over everything again from the last couple of days.

Lawson and Sarah had both been exhausted and the guys had been too wound up to deal with the day's events last night. Everyone needed a clearer head and a good night's rest to process what had happened and come up with their next course of action.

Facing Granger and his men sleep-deprived would do none of them any good in the end.

"In Lawson's defense," Sarah rushed to add, "there was no way to know something like that would happen. We were leaving one minute, then the next, shots were being fired. Lawson did what he had to do to protect us both."

"I thought we could trust Sheriff Willis and his men," Xavier muttered, clearly disappointed. "But if they couldn't even keep those two under lock and key—"

"Hey, now that's not fair," Bailey chimed in. "That is the first time since I started working at the station that something like this has happened. Those two creeps were making all kinds of noise and had everyone uneasy. Everyone—"

"Xavier. They're not used to dealing with people like that," Lawson protested, interrupting Bailey. He didn't want their discussion getting off-track. "They didn't stand a chance. It's a miracle none of them got hurt."

"No, they came right after you," Cade pointed out. "They could have killed you. In the middle of the town square. In front of everyone."

Lawson felt the wound in his side throbbing at him again. It wasn't bad, but it was a reminder of how close he had come to taking a bullet in the gut.

"But they didn't," Lawson replied urgently. "And we don't have time to talk about what might have happened. We've got to focus on what we're going to do now that one of them has gotten away."

"Yeah, and where do we start with that?" Xavier asked. "We don't even know how long it's going to take Paul Donner to get to Granger—"

"Or where he even is," Cade added.

Before Lawson could reply, his phone buzzed in his pocket and he turned away to take the call. The others were so lost in the intensity of their conversation, they hardly even noticed he'd stepped away. He glanced down at the screen: *Unknown number.*

Lainey calling him back?

He'd tossed and turned all night, silently willing her to return his call so he could stop worrying about where she was or what might have happened.

He answered the call, expecting to hear Lainey's voice on the line. But instead, he froze to the spot when he heard a man's smooth, low voice filling his ear instead.

"Lawson Davies," the man said.

He immediately knew whose voice was on the line.

He swallowed hard, but before he could say something in return, Granger spoke again.

"I hear you and your friends have been looking for me," the man continued, his voice calm, unbothered. "I'm a little disappointed that it wasn't more of a challenge to find you. But I'm also delighted to learn a former CIA agent somehow ended up on my tail. I made sure to thank our nosy mutual friend with her help in that."

Granger paused and gave that revelation a moment to settle in Lawson's gut. Then he made a tsking sound, like he was scolding a wayward child, before he continued. "Poor Lainey Daye cracked like an egg. It was such a surprise to come up on her in that small little town. And my man

Paul—the one you had unlawfully arrested—confirmed her whole story before he took his last breath. He was decent help, but he was also responsible for them getting caught and Jim getting killed. I couldn't let that go unpunished."

He chuckled darkly. The sound of it sent a shiver down Lawson's spine. The others seemed to have noticed something was wrong and turned to see what was going on.

"Is Lainey okay? What have you done with her?" Lawson demanded, finally managing to force out the words. He already knew what the answer was going to be.

Granger barked with amusement. "Who do you think I am, Mister Rogers?" he retorted. "No. I'm sorry to report that she is most definitely not okay." He paused briefly. "And for the record, you and your friends won't be, either, when I get my hands on you. I don't appreciate people sticking their damn noses in my business, Mr. Davies."

"If you hurt her—"

"Your words don't mean anything to me," Granger interrupted sharply. "Ms. Daye already understands the repercussions of not minding her own business. However, I will be visiting her again shortly and I'll make sure to give her your regards. Oh, and do say hello to that pretty little therapist of yours, will you? What's her name… Sarah Peterson. I look forward to meeting her soon. Maybe she can help me work out some of my kinks. I bet she's good at that."

And with that, the line went dead. Sheer rage coursed through Lawson's body at the sound of Granger talking about Sarah. He could have crushed the phone in his hand, but he knew he had to keep it together. Behind him, silence filled the room, and he turned to face everyone again.

"Who was that?" Xavier asked, frowning at the phone in Lawson's hand.

Sarah stared at him from the other side of the room, her

face white, as though she had sensed that Granger had been talking about her.

"Granger," he replied bluntly. "He's got Lainey and he made her talk. He knows about us. And the lodge."

"Damn it," Cade muttered, reaching for River and putting his arm around her protectively.

"He's going to be coming here. We need to make preparations," Aaron replied, reaching his hand out toward Bailey. She gripped his hand hard enough that her knuckles turned white and Aaron pulled her to his side.

"What we need to do is get the guests to safety," River replied, pressing into Cade's side for support. "I know what it feels like to be trapped in a place under siege and not knowing if you're going to survive. It's not fair to everyone here to have to go through that."

Sarah walked over to stand beside Lawson, nodding at River to acknowledge her concerns.

"I agree with River. We need to get everyone off the property now," Sarah insisted. "We have a duty to everyone here. We can't let them stay now that Granger knows about the lodge. They'll be sitting ducks. They come here to recover and find peace. They don't deserve to be thrown back into a war."

"No. No way," Xavier replied, shaking his head. "This place is my home. We just got everything almost back to normal. I'm not leaving this place defenseless. I'm not going to be run off it by some two-bit—"

"We don't have a choice, Xavier!" Sarah protested.

"We all live here. It's our home too," Cade gruffly corrected.

"I agree with Xavier. I don't want to go," Hannah replied, her voice filled with anxiety at the situation they faced. "I—

We need to provide stability for everyone who stays here, we can't just kick them out."

"We're not kicking them out," Sarah argued. "Think about it, people. This is supposed to be a place of healing, of safety. We can't provide stability for them if we're..." She trailed off, letting that unspoken word hang in the air between them all. She didn't need to say it out loud—everyone knew what she meant.

"They're right, Xavier, and you know it," Lawson said, stepping forward and nodding. "We can't risk leaving these people here as prey for Granger and his men. Everyone here could be hurt or worse. Do you really want that on your conscious? We need to get them out. Now."

Xavier gritted his teeth and fisted his hands down at his sides. Lawson could tell from just a glance that he was furious at the situation and wanted to put up more of a fight. Lawson couldn't worry about that now, though. Granger and his men would be coming for them soon and he just wanted to get the guests out of here before that happened.

And do everything he could to keep Sarah safe in the process.

Chapter Nineteen

"I don't get it," Chuck protested. "Why do we have to leave?"

"It's just for a few days," Sarah replied quickly. "You'll be back on the property before you know it. Is your stuff packed? We have another car leaving in a half hour."

Chuck crossed his arms over his chest and narrowed his eyes at her. "I'm not going until I get an explanation as to why we have to leave," he said.

Behind him, milling in the entrance hall to the lodge, were a half-dozen other guests who were equally confused as to what was going on. Sarah ran a hand through her hair, trying to pull herself together. She understood their reluctance to leave, especially without really knowing why they were asking them all to go. Unfortunately, though, she didn't have time to offer explanations right now. They were on a tight deadline to get the property cleared…fast. None of them could say for sure when Granger and his men would attack, the guys just knew it was going to be soon and they didn't want to get caught unprepared.

All the staff at the lodge were in the process of moving the guests to a motel in town, where the sheriff said he would have a few of his men standing guard until the threat from Victor Granger was neutralized. It wasn't much, but it was the best they could do for now. Sarah just knew there was no way they could stay here. All of them had been through so much to bring them to Warrior Peak in the first place, and she would never forgive herself if staying at the lodge now brought even more trauma into their lives.

Spinning a story to get them out of here had been tough, though, and Sarah felt guilty for uprooting them from their safe space without a good explanation. She had been trying to coax them into gathering their stuff and leaving, while the other women helped clear out their rooms and a couple of the guys shuttled them to town.

It had been an all-day job so far, and she could feel the exhaustion making her hazy around the edges. She wanted to curl up in bed and sleep, but she doubted she would be able to get any rest, even after all of the guests were safely at the motel.

"There's been a threat against the property," she told him finally. "We need to get you out of here until we can be sure that it's been dealt with."

Chuck's face dropped. There was a murmur of surprise among the other guests. Hopefully, that would be enough to hold them for now, and convince them it wasn't safe for them to be here.

"I'll finish packing up," Chuck muttered, and he rushed back toward his room, followed by the other guests who had overheard. Sarah closed her eyes and leaned back against the door for a moment, breathing a sigh of relief. This was the last group they had to get down to the motel, then the only ones left on the property would be the eight of them. The remaining staff would be staying in town, too.

Not that she imagined it was going to be much easier then, given how much Xavier had been digging in his heels about this. He and Lawson were in the office right now arguing. She'd passed by a half hour ago and heard raised voices, but she understood it. Though it was home to all of them, Xavier was the most attached to this place. It had, after all, been his family's property before they'd turned it into Warrior Peak Sanctuary. He had to feel like he was losing part of himself and his past by leaving the lodge to be threatened, possibly even destroyed, by Granger and his men.

Sarah shivered when she thought about that evil man, and when she remembered the look Lawson had given her when he had gotten off that call with him. His eyes had landed on her immediately for a moment, and she had known without him having to say anything that Granger had said something about her.

Finally, when the last group of guests were shuttled out of the lodge, Sarah stepped outside to the porch and inhaled a big lungful of fresh air. It was nearly ten, and she could feel the raw exhaustion getting the better of her. From the moment the sound of gunfire had first filled the air in the town square yesterday, she hadn't had a moment to pull herself together. She wasn't even sure if she could at this point.

Especially with so much tension between the guys in the lodge right now. None of them had eaten all day, and she doubted that was helping much with their frazzled nerves. She had thought about going to the kitchen to cook something up, but with how shaky she was right now, she wouldn't have trusted herself around a hot stove.

She stared off to the edge of the property, where the trees that lined the horse paddocks in the distance had started to cast long shadows on the ground below. She shivered as she looked at the trees. They would provide good cover for someone looking to sneak up on them. She could almost feel eyes on her now, like Granger and his men were watching her from the shadows, ready to make their move at any moment.

"Hey."

She nearly jumped out of her skin when she heard a voice behind her. Turning, she saw it was Lawson.

"Oh, it's you," she murmured, sighing with relief.

He nodded, stepping out on to the porch behind her and slipping his arms around her waist. "Sorry to scare you," he said, placing a kiss on the side of her neck.

She closed her eyes, trying to let the comfort of his presence ground her some. It did, a little. It seemed like a miracle that anything could break through the weight of the fear in her system right now, but Lawson could.

"You finally get Xavier to agree with you?" she asked him, and he let out a small chuckle.

"The day I get Xavier to admit he's wrong about something is the day hell freezes over," he said wryly. "I don't think I'll ever manage that. But he's not fighting me on it anymore, at least. He's with Hannah right now. Calming her down."

"She okay?"

"As much as she can be." He sighed. "I don't think any of us are exactly at the top of our game currently."

Sarah leaned against him and nodded in agreement. Right now, it felt as though they were on the eve of war, just waiting for the battle call to sound. It would be a miracle if they all made it out of this in one piece. Tensions were high, and everyone was scared, but dealing with it in their own way.

"Have you checked in with Sheriff Willis?" she asked him, and she felt him sigh against her neck.

"I tried to get through to him, but all the lines are busy and our cell phones don't seem to be working, either."

She turned to him, her brow furrowed. "Why do you think that is?"

"I think it's Granger trying to isolate us," he admitted. "This is his way of making sure we can't get anyone up here to help us."

"I guess it's a good thing that you spoke to the sheriff earlier when you were arranging protection for the guests. At least he's aware of what's happening up here."

"Yes, he's aware. He was dealing with the FBI when I spoke to him. Handling the Donner and Adams situation. And as soon as he's done, they'll all be heading this way." Sarah breathed a sigh of relief from his words.

"That's good news, then. Do you think they'll make it up here in time to help?" she asked hopefully.

Lawson searched her face, like he was committing her features to memory. "I'm not sure, but it would be great if they did. At least we know they'll be coming. Sarah…"

He stopped talking, and stared at her for a long moment. She knew, before he said anything, what was going to come out of his mouth. She had been ready for it, from the moment they had started moving people off the property.

"I need you to go, too, Sarah," he told her gently.

She shook her head. She had been preparing what she was going to say to him since that morning. She could help them at the lodge, and she'd rather be in danger with the people she cared about than safe and alone, wondering what was happening.

"No. I need to be here," she replied firmly. "With you. And the other women, they need me. I know this place, I can be a help—"

"Sarah. You know you can't stay. It's too dangerous. I can't focus on what needs to be done if I'm worried about you," he pointed out. "I care too much about you to have you here when all hell breaks loose. I'd never be able to forgive myself if something happens to you."

Those words knocked the breath from her lungs. She knew exactly what he meant. It felt like such a twisted joke, for all of this to have happened now that they were together. It was so unfair.

"I can't leave you, Lawson," she breathed, and he closed his eyes, resting his forehead against hers for a moment.

"I don't want to be apart from you, Sarah, believe me," he murmured. "But I need to have a clear head going into this. And I can only have that if you're safely away from here. You need to go with the other women, and you can look out for each other. Bailey knows how to handle herself. You'll be safe with her."

She gazed at him. She knew there would be no changing his mind, but she still asked him one last time to reconsider.

"I don't want to leave you to take this on alone," she protested, even though she was certain it was futile.

"I'm not going to be alone," he assured her. "I have the best damn backup in the country. If anyone can end this, you know it's going to be us."

She smiled slightly. Well, he had a point there. Victor Granger might be scary, but he didn't know what he was dealing with—three former military, two being former CIA, too, and a former cop. Or the other things the past couple of years they'd had to face down together.

"Will you please go?" he asked her. "For me?"

"Yes, I'll go," she replied. "But promise me something, Lawson. Promise me you're not going to do anything crazy."

He kissed her, the kind of urgent, needy kiss that told her just how high the stakes were.

She grabbed his face, holding him there longer, not wanting this moment to be over.

He pulled back and smiled at her, a little sadly.

"You know I can't promise that," he replied. "Come on, pack your stuff. You need to leave."

Chapter Twenty

Lawson lifted a hand to wave off Sarah and the rest of the women, who were departing the lodge in Bailey's car. His heart twisted in his chest as he stared at Sarah, the sadness at leaving written all over her face. He wouldn't have expected anything less, but as long as she was going and would be safe, that was all he could ask for right now.

He thought she'd put up more of a fight to stay, but she seemed to understand how important it was that she left with the others.

When Granger had made that threat against her, Lawson knew there wasn't a chance in hell he could have kept her here without being out of his mind with worry the entire time. He wouldn't be able to focus and it would end up costing them all.

As soon as the car was out of sight, he turned to the team of men behind him—Cade, Aaron and Xavier stood next to the door, each of them with a grim expression on their face. They knew they were about to take on the fight of their lives, and whether they made it out in one piece was going to be down to their skills and their instincts. With their women safe, they could now focus on taking down Granger. For good.

"Come on, let's get geared up," Lawson instructed them.

He had taken the lead, as he always did at the lodge. It was his tactical unit and he knew he couldn't let any of them think he had any doubts about how this was going to go. Sometimes being a good leader meant showing confidence you might not really feel in order to keep your team strong, assured and focused.

The guys headed inside to the dining room, where they had gathered everything they had in the way of weaponry and firepower—well, what was left after setting the various traps around the property.

In silence, the guys got themselves ready—guns holstered, bulletproof vests on, knives strapped to their thighs and various other smaller ones on their bodies. The air was crackling with tension as the reality of what they were preparing for set in, and Lawson could tell they were all lost in thought. Probably thinking about their women, and wondering if they would really survive this. Just like Lawson was.

"We have the home-field advantage," Lawson reminded them, and the guys lifted their heads to look at him. "Remember that. It's the biggest bonus we have on our side, and we have to use it against them."

"You think Granger's going to make his move tonight?" Xavier asked.

Lawson nodded. "I can't see why he wouldn't," he replied. "He knows that he has us right where he wants us and he's already cut off our communication. The faster he strikes, the less time he gives us to prepare. And he's arrogant. He thinks he can easily take us down."

Cade nodded, sliding a serrated knife into a thigh sheath.

"But his arrogance can easily be his undoing," Lawson went on. "He's used to having the upper hand. All his lackeys are scared of him, their fear rules them. And he's accustomed to having that kind of control. If we can lure him out here, get him on our territory, it might be enough to throw him off."

Might be being the crucial part of that, though he didn't say it out loud. All of them were thinking it, but the last thing they needed was to start letting their nerves get the better of them. If their confidence wavered for a single minute, all of this would be over before it really even started, and there was no way Lawson was going to let Victor Granger and his men win that easily.

When he thought of everything they had been through, everything they had survived up until this moment, he knew he couldn't—wouldn't—let the other man win. They had fought too hard for this place, to make it safe for the people who needed it, and he would be damned if he allowed that evil man to take it from them.

Which was why the guys had spent the better part of the last hour setting up traps all around the property. Trip wires that would trigger flash-bangs, grenades and smoke bombs. Enough to give the guys a warning as to where they were approaching from. These guys were criminals, at the end of the day, and likely hadn't dealt much with enemies who had tactical knowledge like Lawson and his friends. Granger and his men didn't know what they were up against.

"How many do you think there are going to be?" Aaron asked.

Lawson grimaced. "I don't know exactly," he admitted. "But I would guess somewhere in the realm of twenty or thirty. I doubt Granger will be able to move all of his men out here on such short notice, but he likely travels with a large crew in case of situations like this..." He trailed off.

A crew, he had to admit, who had Lainey. If she was even still alive. He hadn't been able to hear her voice on his call with Granger, and Lawson had a bad feeling that the man had either killed her or hurt her badly. Men like Granger didn't like leaving loose ends. Especially ones that caused him trouble and brought attention to him and his operation. He cursed himself for not being more careful, not keeping a closer eye on her, but it was too late for that now.

Right now, they just had to deal with the threat in front of them. If they were able to take down these guys, then hopefully, Lawson would be able to get Lainey out of his clutches and back to her family.

He pushed down those thoughts. No distractions. He couldn't let his emotions get the better of him. If there was one thing he had learned from his time in the field, it was that the people who let their hearts get in the way of their heads usually ended up dead as a result.

Lawson looked around at his friends. If he had to take on a man like Victor Granger and his crew, he was damn glad he was doing it with these men standing beside him. After all the time they'd spent together over the years, working together, trusting each other, becoming a team. He would do everything in his power to make sure they all walked away in one piece.

"Thank you for standing with me on this," he told them gruffly. He wasn't good at saying what was on his mind at the best of times, but now, he needed them to know how much confidence he had in them.

"I know there's only four of us, but we can do this," he continued, as Cade, Aaron and Xavier nodded. "We have the advantage. And they have no idea what they're coming up against. We can win this. I know we can."

"You ready to do this?" Xavier asked, and Lawson nodded. He reached for the control panel next to the door and pulled the switch. The whole property was plunged into an eerie darkness.

"Let's do this," Cade said.

"I'm ready," Aaron answered.

"Then let's get into position," Lawson replied. "Cade, Aaron—upstairs, split up. Each of you take a side. You'll have the advantage through the upper windows to see out over more of the property. Take the front side. Concentrate on taking them out before they get close enough to infiltrate the lodge. You got your rifles?"

They both held them up.

"Good," he replied. "Xavier and I will cover the downstairs windows, out the back. Okay, guys, let's move."

They got into position. Xavier and Lawson crouched in different areas at the windows that looked out toward the back of the property. Any minute now, they knew the place would be lit up by some sort of explosion, and then their fight would truly start. But, for now, they had to hold out in silence, waiting for something to happen.

"You ever thought this was how it would go?" Xavier muttered to him wryly. "When we opened this place?"

Lawson chuckled, glad for something to break the tension.

"I had a lot of plans for the lodge, but this wasn't in them," he admitted. "What about you?"

Xavier shook his head. "Same," he replied. "Not exactly how I pictured it going. But I guess we should have known our pasts would come back to haunt us."

"This is where it ends," Lawson replied firmly. "After this, we'll implement some new safety procedures and protocols so the lodge will never come under threat again."

Xavier glanced at him out of the corner of his eye.

"Guess you've got more to protect now, too, huh?" he remarked.

Lawson nodded, his mind flashing once more to Sarah. He was glad she left with the other women, but at the same time, he wished she was beside him. When she was close, it was like everything else just fell into place. Even though he knew he had made the right choice by asking her to leave, he missed her already.

"Yeah, I guess I do," he replied.

"You think we'll get backup in time?" Xavier asked, glancing at his watch, then looking out the window across the yard.

Lawson grunted. "Wish I could say yes, but I think we'll mostly be on our own. The sheriff and FBI had a lot to wrap up, so I guess it really depends on how long it takes them to do everything they need done."

"Maybe the women will get to town and let Willis know what's happening. That they've blocked our communications. That should help speed up the assistance," Xavier offered while moving to another window.

Both of them fell silent again, ears straining for any sound outside. Upstairs, there was a creak on the floorboards. Cade and Aaron were getting into position to look out over the grounds.

"Remember, don't show them any mercy," Lawson told Xavier, shifting back to battle mode. "You know they wouldn't give any to us. We need to strike hard and fast. Take out as many as we can, as fast as possible. If we're lucky, they'll hit some of the traps first and that will help improve our odds."

Xavier nodded. Lawson knew he didn't need to tell him twice. He was gripping the gun in his holster tightly, ready to take a shot at a moment's notice, but there was still nothing. After a few more seconds of silence, the grounds lit up in a burst of light. An explosion echoed from the right side of the lodge.

"Here we go. Let's get it done."

Chapter Twenty-One

Sarah stared out of the window as the last view of the lodge disappeared out of sight. Bailey had just pulled off the property and onto the winding mountain road that would lead them down to Blue Ridge. Sarah's stomach tightened with worry, praying they would make the hour drive to town unscathed.

Normally, going for a drive made Sarah feel so free and alive—the wind in her hair, feeling the sunlight on her face, and the smell of clean forest air wafting through the windows. But tonight, under cover of darkness and fear, she felt as though the car's exterior was shrinking around her.

She didn't want to leave Lawson, and she could tell the other women with her felt the same. How could they just up and drive away from the men they loved? Even if it was for the best, it felt wrong. Logically, Sarah knew Lawson was right. She and the other women, except Bailey, would be a hinderance to the men. They'd be a distraction, splitting their focus and possibly getting someone killed. That was the last thing she wanted on her conscious. She'd never forgive herself if she was the cause of one of her friends being hurt, or worse. But her heart? Her heart was demanding she return and stand by his side. Help protect him as he would protect her. As senseless as it sounded, that's all she wanted to do.

"I can't believe we have to leave," River muttered, breaking the silence as she stared out of the window.

"It won't be for long," Sarah assured her, slipping at once into therapist mode. "And we all know it's for the best. We want the guys to be able to focus on what they need to do instead of worrying about us, right?"

"Exactly," Bailey agreed. She had that confident tone to her voice that made Sarah start to unwind slightly. If there was anyone she could trust with all of this, it was Bailey. She had a good head on her shoulders, and she knew exactly how to handle herself in situations like this. After all, Bailey was a cop down in Blue Ridge. Sarah was thankful for that knowledge.

"We have to concentrate on what's in our control right now, not what's out of it," Sarah continued. There was something comforting about sliding into this familiar role, telling them what she knew they needed to hear. It might not be easy, keeping calm when she felt so terrified, but she knew they needed to stick together to make it through this.

"Yeah, agreed," Bailey replied. "The guys are relying on us to keep ourselves safe. That's what we need to do right now."

Hannah was sitting in the passenger seat, staring silently out the window like she couldn't even hear them. River had her arms wrapped around herself and was shivering slightly. They were all dealing with their fears in their own ways, but Sarah hated seeing her friends so lost and upset. She gritted her teeth. She needed to stay strong, and pass that strength on to the other women.

They would all survive this. Their men would be fine. And they'd all be together again soon.

"We're going to be back at the lodge tomorrow," Bailey announced as though she could sense the tension in the car. "And Granger and his goons are going to be where they belong. Behind bars."

Sarah noticed how tightly Bailey's hands gripped the wheel as she spoke and how her eyes constantly checked the review mirror, looking for danger. Of all the women in the car, this had to be worse for her. With Bailey being a cop and having the knowledge and skills she did, it had to be hard for her to be there escorting the women instead of helping their men defend their home.

Sarah tried to think of something positive she could add to Bailey's words. Something that might help ease the tension but nothing came to mind. Normally, she had many reassurances she offered her clients in times of stress, but right now her mind was blank. Her thoughts buried behind her own unease and terror.

All at once, Sarah stiffened as headlights appeared behind them. Bailey's eyes suddenly darted to the rearview mirror.

"Was there anyone else coming down from the lodge?" she asked, concerned.

Sarah shook her head. "Not that I know of. We should have been the last ones to leave."

"Well, there's another car—"

"Bailey, look out!"

River screamed just in time to alert Bailey to the car heading directly for them up the mountain road. Bailey slammed her foot on the brake and twisted the wheel to avoid a head-on collision, sending them grinding into the dirt and grass at the side of the road. Sarah jerked forward, grabbing the back of Hannah's seat in front of her to hold herself steady.

Bailey cursed to herself as she glanced around, trying to figure out what they should do. The bright lights behind them suddenly revealed another vehicle slowing to a stop a short distance away.

There was no way out. One car blocked the road heading down the mountain, and another blocked their way back to the lodge.

They were trapped.

River whimpered and hugged herself tighter, Hannah sat frozen in her seat and Bailey and Sarah were each watching a set of headlights, waiting to see what would happen next.

Sarah's stomach twisted in fear. It had to be Granger or some of his men. They must have already been watching the lodge while everyone was planning to leave, waiting for the perfect time to strike.

They were too far away from the lodge now, for Lawson or the others to know they needed help. Besides, if these cars were here, Sarah was sure they were at the lodge too. Help wouldn't be coming for them. They would get out of this on their own. One way or another.

The vehicle behind them was a black SUV with dark-tinted windows, making it nearly impossible to see anyone inside. The women sat in terrified silence and waited as the front passenger door opened, and a well-dressed man stepped out. The moment Sarah laid eyes on him, she knew he had to be Victor Granger.

There was nobody else who would have carried themselves like that, she was sure of it. He exuded a cold, calculated confidence. His head was shaven, and his face radiated a fury Sarah had never seen before. She felt like a helpless animal trapped by a ferocious predator, ready to swallow her whole.

Granger made his way toward the car, and his eyes

seemed pinned to Sarah's. He gave her a dark, cruel grin that sent a shiver down her spine. But it told her exactly what she needed to know. He was there for her, not any of the other women. He had singled out Sarah with that one look. Now, she could use that knowledge to her advantage and get the others out of there.

She quickly turned to the other women, lowering her voice and speaking urgently.

"Listen to me," she ordered them. "He's here for me. He's trying to get leverage over Lawson, I'm sure of it. If I make a break for it, then he's going to send his men after me. And you can get out of here."

"We're not leaving you here," Bailey said sharply, sounding angry at the very suggestion.

River and Hannah shook their heads emphatically to agree with Bailey.

"You're leaving for me, because I'm asking you to," Sarah assured them. "You all need to get to safety, then you can get me help. But you have to get out of here in order to do that."

"Sarah, no." Hannah reached back and grabbed her hand.

"There is no way this car is leaving without you in it. I will not leave you here for these men. Lawson is depending on me keeping you safe, Sarah. I won't do it," Bailey said, all but growling at her.

"It's the only way, and you three know it. He won't hurt me, he'll take me back to the lodge to flaunt me at Lawson. To show him he couldn't keep me safe. When I make a run for it, you need to hurry. He won't be expecting it, you can get away. I can't..."

Her voice hitched at the back of her throat as the reality of this situation began to sink in. She was going to have to get out of this car and put herself in grave danger, to ensure her friends could get away. The thought was terrifying. But she knew it was the only way to help her friends. To give them a chance.

It seemed Granger had been making his own plans on how best to get to Lawson, throw him off his game. Apparently, she was his trump card. The man knew Lawson would do anything to keep her out of harm's way, and that would most likely get him and the other guys at the lodge killed. Sarah couldn't let herself be used like that. Against the man she loved.

Granger stopped a short distance from her side of the car, holding his hands up, trying to seem nonthreatening.

"Sarah Peterson, my dear," he said with a smile curling his lips. "We've been looking for you everywhere."

She reached for the door handle, her heart pounding in her chest. River shot her a panicked look and squeezed her leg tightly, as though telling her to stay right where she was, but she knew she couldn't. She couldn't risk her friends getting caught, too.

Hannah turned in her seat and pinned Sarah with her watery eyes. "Sarah, please—please don't do this. We need to stay together."

Sarah shook head and turned to Bailey, giving her a hard look.

"You need to get out of here, get to Sheriff Willis," she firmly told her.

"Sarah—" Bailey replied, but Sarah just cut her off.

"Bailey. You know this is the right move. Get to town as fast as you can."

Bailey gritted her teeth and took a deep breath, then nodded and pinned Sarah with a determined gaze. "Fine. We'll go," she replied. She seemed to know as well as Sarah did that there was no other way out of this. She would do her part, and she had to trust that her friends would do theirs.

"You stay alive out there. Lawson will kill me if anything happens to you. You hear me?"

For Lawson. For her friends. She had to run. She had to put as much distance between herself and these men as she could. She doubted she would be able to outrun them, but she was going to give it everything she had.

Sarah sucked in a deep breath, trying to slow the terror gripping her insides, then nodded once to acknowledge Bailey's demand. "I will."

Then she threw open the door and bolted into the trees, heading back up toward the lodge.

"After her!" Granger roared, and Sarah heard doors being thrown open, heavy footfalls behind her. Her heart slammed against her ribs and her breath tore from her lungs, the humid summer air already starting to make her sweat.

She didn't exactly know where she was going, she just knew she was pointed in the general direction of the lodge and she had to get as far from these men as she could. She ran with everything she had, even though her legs were like rubber beneath her. She forced herself to keep moving.

She heard men's voices calling after her, and the squeal of tires on the pavement. She prayed her friends would get away. Get to town and get help and rescue her before anything horrible happened. She was sure a man like Victor Granger wouldn't think twice about using the other women as leverage, too, and the thought of something happening to them… It made her sick to think about it.

Twigs snapped beneath her feet as she ran, as she darted away from the trees and back toward the road, knowing she would only get lost in these dark woods. She felt the same fear she had on that fateful day back in her office with Jed, when everything had fallen apart as she watched his vicious destruction. All the safety she'd felt up to that point was suddenly ripped away. She was now faced with the brutal reality of how much danger she was in.

She just needed to make it to the lodge, to Lawson.

She curled her hands into fists, arms pumping through the air, pushing her legs as fast as they would go as she heard cars on the road behind her. She glanced around to see Bailey's car closing the distance between them. Damn it, she'd hoped Bailey would take her advice and get help, but at the same time, there was a part of her that was beyond relieved that her friends hadn't left her after all.

"Sarah! Get in!" Bailey yelled to her as she drove alongside Sarah. Sarah reached out for the car door, but missed. Sarah cried out in frustration. She was too slow and they were too fast; they couldn't make another pass or slow down for fear of being caught. There was another car closing the distance behind them.

And then, she felt a pressure at her back. Someone grabbed her shirt and pulled her back toward them. She screamed out in surprise and tried to break free, but the grip was too strong. There was no way she could escape.

Sarah was yanked to a halt and fell back to the ground. All of the adrenaline she had coursing through her veins suddenly fled, and her body felt like a sinking weight in quicksand. This was the end for her. She was well and truly caught, and she had no clue what would happen next. Tears suddenly blurred her vision and she let out a terror-filled scream that cut through the night air.

Dark, shiny shoes suddenly stopped in front of her, and she shrank back, bumping into the legs of the man behind her.

"Stand her up." A low, menacing voice practically growled the words. Two sets of rough hands grabbed her and pulled her to her feet.

She stood there, surrounded by several men, her panicked gaze darting around until it landed on their leader.

Victor Granger.

She waited for what he would say. Would he order her killed? Or keep her to use against Lawson?

Out of the corner of her eye she saw Bailey's car race by with Hannah's and River's faces plastered against the windows, eyes wide in fear for her. At least her friends got away. Sarah had no clue what would happen next, but she knew she had to be strong. For the same reasons she had to run—for Lawson, for her friends—she had to survive.

Chapter Twenty-Two

Flash-bangs and men's startled yells sounded around the lodge from Granger's men trying to breach the perimeter of the property. From the sounds and multiple bright lights, Lawson knew they were surrounded and the first wave of men were closing in. He glanced at Xavier to see him peer out the window, seeking his first target. Lawson repositioned himself, lifted his weapon and looked out to find his own.

Just as Lawson locked on the first man breaching the trees, a terrified scream rent the air, causing the hairs on his neck to stand on end. Every muscle in Lawson's body tensed.

He looked over at Xavier, checking to see if he'd heard it, too. Xavier's eyes were wide. And he looked just as worried as Lawson about what that sound meant.

Whose voice that had been. But Lawson knew.

He was on his feet before he could argue with himself. He knew better than to do what he was about to do. He should stick to the plan, no matter what. But there was no way he could ignore that agonizing, terror-filled scream.

He knew beyond a doubt that that scream was Sarah. He couldn't leave her to face whatever Granger had planned for her alone.

Xavier grabbed his arm and pulled him back down, and Lawson tried to shake himself free. He couldn't think about the plans they'd put in place or how much danger he'd be putting himself in by going out there. He had to make sure Sarah was safe. It was the only thing he cared about.

"You can't go out there," Xavier warned him. "The plan's in motion. None of it is going to work if you blow this for us now, you know that."

Lawson gritted his teeth. He knew Xavier was right, but he had to make sure Sarah was okay. He knew he shouldn't have let her leave without him. He should have escorted her to town, then come back to face off with Granger. Now, with more worry for her on his mind, he didn't know if he'd be able to clear his head enough to focus on what he had to do.

"It could have been anything," Xavier told him, his face grim, and Lawson knew what he was not saying. He was reminding Lawson that it was as likely to be Hannah as it was Sarah, that all of the men had loved ones out there tonight. But Victor was relying on them losing their cool, and they had too much riding on this to let that happen.

Lawson crouched down beside the window again, that scream ringing in his ears. Granger must have ambushed them leaving and grabbed Sarah. So what did that mean for his sister and the other two women? He knew Granger would have singled out Sarah because of him. He even implied as much when he'd called Lawson to boast about Lainey.

But before he could linger on that thought any longer, a sharp explosion of light filled the sky. Another flash-bag, at the front of the lodge.

Aaron spoke through his comm a moment later.

"Six men coming up the driveway," he told them. "Flash-bang has them staggering about blindly."

"Take them out," Lawson replied without a second thought. A moment later, gunfire filled the air, breaking through the silence, echoing through the quiet night—the men were being picked off with ease.

"More are coming," Aaron warned them. "You guys ready?"

"Roger that," the other three men replied in their comms simultaneously.

Another flash-bang went off at the opposite edge of the property, and Xavier and Lawson ducked down beneath the windows on the ground floor, both of them leveling their weapons, ready to take the shot whenever they could. There were several more men staggering around, trying to regain their sight, weapons dangling from their shoulders or hands. They needed to deal with these men now, before their vision cleared and they could return fire.

Lawson lined up his weapon, and fired: one, two, three. He'd picked off three guys in a row, while Xavier took out the other two. Bodies littered the front and back of the property, and Lawson knew it was far from over.

"How many more do you think we're going to be dealing with?" Xavier asked as he steadied his gun on the sill of the open window before him.

Lawson shook his head. "I have no idea," he replied, voice tight with worry. He still couldn't clear the scream from his mind, even in the midst of a gunfight.

His thoughts kept circling back to the women and what Granger would possibly do. He knew the man would want to use Sarah against him, force his hand to surrender. But what about the others? Bailey was a cop and she had her gun. Had he captured them—or worse?

All at once, several rounds of gunfire sounded from the front of the lodge, jolting Lawson back to the present. One of the windows behind them smashed, exploding inward in a hail of glass and bullets. Xavier and Lawson dropped down on instinct, not making themselves any more of a target than they needed to be.

He heard Cade's voice over the comm about several more men approaching, followed by more gunfire, then the sounds of men yelling and thuds of bodies hitting the ground outside. Good. They were clearing these guys out quickly.

Lawson couldn't help wondering how many more men Granger would end up sacrificing to get his hands on him. Would he continue until his last man? Or would he realize it was hopeless and give up or make a run for it?

A loud boom drew Lawson's attention, and he spun around, ducking below the window. A couple of guys had been blown off their feet and one was scrambling for cover while the second lay unmoving on the ground. Xavier took the shot and took the man out before he made it far. At the same time, they heard more windows being shattered and more gunfire sounding from outside. Those men were determined to get in, no matter what it took or how many lives were lost in the process.

Cade and Aaron were also consistently firing from the second floor. Every once in a while, one of them would make a mumbled comment over their comms, but with all the noise and explosions, it was hard to make out most of what they were saying. He and Xavier just had to rely on the fact that Cade and Aaron were both skilled with weapons and would have each other's backs with whatever came at them. If they really needed help, they'd definitely let Lawson and Xavier know they were in trouble.

Lawson turned his attention back outside. Both men had their weapons balanced in the window, waiting for anything that moved in the darkness.

"There," Xavier muttered, pointing out a dark figure

moving at the edge of the grounds. "You see him? He's next to the path—"

"Got him," Lawson replied, and he fired a shot. It smashed off the concrete path below, and the man sprang to the side, dodging the bullet. Lawson cursed, and quickly reloaded, lining up another shot.

He exhaled as he pulled the trigger, squeezing down on it in time with his breath, and this time, the shot landed, hitting the man in the leg. He let out a howl of pain that filled the air around them, and Lawson let out a sigh of relief. Thank God. He couldn't get sloppy, not now, when every shot could mean life or death for him and his friends.

Silence filled the air once more, then another flash of light from outside. Aaron and Cade picked off the few who were approaching from the front of the lodge, and Lawson ran over to one of the shattered windows to get a better look at what was happening. There had to be at least twelve dead by now, maybe even more. Granger couldn't have many more men with him to send in now.

"How many more does he have?" he muttered almost to himself, running a hand through his hair.

"We must have evened the playing field a little by now," Xavier agreed. Lawson could hear the hope in his voice.

"I'm not sure. It'd be nice if this was almost over but it's doubtful. We haven't seen Granger yet. So he must have something else up his sleeve for us," Lawson added.

And Lawson couldn't help but think that it had to do with that scream. And Sarah. Granger had singled her out when he'd called Lawson to boast about finding them, so he knew the man would make a play for her at some point. That was why Lawson had wanted her down in town instead of there with him. There was no way to know for sure, though, until it was all over. And Granger played his final hand.

A long quiet surrounded them, as they waited for the next attack to come. But it didn't. Lawson and Xavier glanced around the property again, looking for movement, but everything was calm outside.

"Clear up here, for now. You guys good?" Cade's question crackled over the comm.

"Good here," Xavier replied warily.

Lawson and Xavier glanced at each other, concern crossing both their faces. Was this it? Had Granger decided to change tactics and leave instead? Move to another location and use these men as decoys while he got away free and clear? Not the best-case scenario because he'd still be out there preying on the unsuspecting and vulnerable, but at least Lawson and his team would be free of the danger surrounding them. They could step back and let the FBI take over.

What about Lainey, though? Lawson's gut clenched at the thought of his friend. She'd been a constant worry in the back of his mind and he felt guilty he hadn't tried to find her yet. He wanted to keep his promise, to get her back to her family. For them to all be safe. First, he had to deal with the immediate danger to him and his friends. To Sarah. Then he'd focus all his attention and resources on finding Lainey and bringing her home.

All at once, the comms crackled to life again.

"Heads up," Aaron warned them. "There's a car down the main road, looks like it's headed toward the lodge. And it doesn't look like Bailey's."

"It's Granger," Xavier stated. "Has to be."

Both Lawson and Xavier rechecked their weapons, readying themselves for the next round. Lawson called through his comm for Cade and Aaron to do the same. He wanted them all to be loaded up and ready for whatever came next.

With Victor Granger's arrival, this would be it. The final

showdown. Lawson and Xavier shared a look of determination. They were ready to do whatever was necessary to protect the lodge and their women, including putting themselves on the line. Their women's safety and happiness were all that mattered to them in the end.

Chapter Twenty-Three

Sarah couldn't stop staring at Victor Granger's hand on her knee. He'd placed it there the moment she had been pulled into his car, making it clear to her that there was no way she was going anywhere. As if she didn't know that already. She felt like she was going to throw up. Her entire body was wracked with tension and fear as she continued to stare at his hand.

She glanced out of the window and realized they were on the connector road to the lodge. At the rate of speed the man behind the wheel was driving, they'd be there in a few minutes. She'd be able to see Lawson. A part of her was relieved that she would be able to see him again. But another part of her was terrified at what Granger would do to her as soon as he had her in front of Lawson once more.

"I can't wait to see the look on his face," the man in the front seat said as he smirked in amusement. "That ex-CIA bastard, he's going to see what he gets when he messes with us—"

"Shut your mouth, Lyle," Granger told him bluntly. It was clear he was not in the mood to listen to the younger man's gloating. "I'll do the talking. Keep your thoughts to yourself."

The man's face fell, and he turned back to look out the

windshield, concentrating on the road in front of him. The man beside him in the driver's seat, who looked just like him, let out a snort of amusement.

"Shut up, Nelson," Lyle mumbled to his look-alike, then punched him on the shoulder.

Sarah gripped the door handle tightly, wondering if she could throw open the door and jump out and escape. But she knew the car was going too fast and she wouldn't survive.

Even if Granger and these other men were going to flaunt her capture in front of Lawson before they decided what to do with her, at least she'd be able to see the man she loved again.

Sarah knew the women would have driven down to Blue Ridge by now to alert the sheriff, but she had no idea if the cavalry would make it back up to the lodge in time to save her or help end the attack. She just wanted all of this to be over.

She wished everything could go back as it was before they were aware of the kidnappings and Granger's arrival in the area. Everything had been so chaotic lately, Sarah couldn't even recall what a normal day was supposed to be like for her now. It all just felt so hopeless.

For a moment, Sarah even thought about trying to reason with the man beside her.

She could tell him that Lawson was a good man, and that he just wanted Granger and his operation out of the area. That Lawson would look the other way, leave him to his business, if he just left the lodge and its people alone. No harm, no foul.

She could try to feed him all those lies, but she knew she wouldn't be very convincing. And he'd never believe her, if she tried. He'd probably laugh in her face. Lawson never would have looked the other way when it came to what Granger was up to, not in a million years. He wanted to see the man behind bars, maybe even dead. If that was what it took to get him out of the picture.

Sarah shut down those thoughts at once. She couldn't believe she was actually considering bargaining with the evil man sitting beside her.

Granger grinned at the side of her face, but Sarah refused to so much as glance in his direction. Instead, she kept her eyes trained out the front windshield. She wasn't going to give him the satisfaction of knowing he had gotten under her skin in any way. She was sure that was part of his plan.

He might be used to getting everything he wanted, but that didn't mean she was going to hand it to him without a fight. She clenched her jaw in determination as they drew closer to the lodge, praying that Lawson was ready for whatever was about to happen.

"He's going to be ready for you," she told them, the first thing she'd said since she had been bundled into the back of this car. The confidence in her voice caught even her off guard, and she finally looked at Granger, who seemed slightly thrown by the way she spoke to him. Apparently, he seemed to expect her to be scared and cowering away from him instead of speaking her mind.

"I hope he is," he replied, quickly gathering himself again. "I want to see the look on his face when he sees that I've got his girlfriend, and when he hears the plans I've got in store for you."

"You're going to make us a pretty penny, Sarah," Lyle told her, grinning at her. There was something lecherous about the way he looked at her, and she couldn't help but shiver. She tried not to let her mind stray too far down that path. She didn't want them to see how afraid she really was.

"Us?" She couldn't help but ask the question. Were the two look-alikes related to Granger?

"Oh, forgive my rudeness," Granger replied cordially. "These are my sons, Lyle and Nelson. They help with certain areas of my operation."

"A family business. What a wonderful role model," she muttered under her breath.

Granger's grip tightened on her knee, causing her to wince. "You've got a smart mouth. You should watch your words before they get you into more trouble."

"You're not going to make a cent from me," she told them, ignoring the man's threat. "You should turn around now. Get out of here while you still can. Hand yourselves over to the cops and hope they take it easy on you."

Lyle and Nelson laughed, but their father, for a moment, was quiet. Had she struck a nerve? She stole a glance at him out of the corner of her eye, but he wasn't giving anything away. He just watched her with his dark, soulless eyes.

Finally, they reached the entrance to the lodge. Sarah couldn't help the gasp that escaped her lips at the sight before her. Smoke still lingered in the air like a thick fog and the ground was littered with bodies. She clenched her hands into fists and her stomach dropped. *Please, please, let those be Granger's men.*

As the car slowed down more, and some of the fog began to clear, she could see what looked like a dozen men on the ground around them—some of them dead, unmoving, others dragging themselves along the ground to safety.

Granger cursed under his breath, then rolled down his window and yelled to them. "Hold your positions!"

His voice was cold, hard, but she could hear the hint of uncertainty behind his words, as though he hadn't been prepared for this sight to greet him when he arrived.

Suddenly, hope rose in her chest. They really were doing it. Lawson and the others were really defending the lodge and taking down Granger's men. The proof was right before their eyes. She hated that she'd had any doubt, but with the army of men they'd been facing against their mere four, she couldn't help but feel the initial helplessness of it all. But now, maybe, just maybe, the guys could end this.

"Stop here," he ordered Nelson, and the vehicle jerked to a hard stop. Sarah clung to the handle of the door, praying that this would be over soon. If she could just find a way to get away from this evil man and his sons…

Granger reached over her and pushed open the door, then shoved her out onto the gravel. She gasped and tumbled to the ground, unprepared, putting her hands out to catch her fall. Gravel bit into her palms as she landed, tearing her skin.

Granger climbed out of the vehicle behind her and grabbed her arm, yanking her to her feet, and held her in front of him like a shield. He must have known Lawson would be quick to take the shot if given the chance, but with Sarah standing in front of the man, he was probably more cautious to do so.

"Lawson Davies!" Granger yelled, his voice booming in her ears. She winced and squeezed her eyes shut at the sound. She wanted to wrench herself away from him, but he had too tight of a hold on her for her to move. She was going to have to bide her time and look for an opening she could use to get away.

"Davies, can you hear me? I've got your woman out here!" he continued, clearly enjoying the power he held in that moment. "You better show yourself unless you want something to happen to her." Granger paused, lifting some of her hair and running his fingers through it. "Nice and silky, and she smells good, too. I bet I could make good money off her. I've got plenty of clients who'd pay well for a chance to take her to bed."

Sarah shuddered at the thought, fear and anger coursing through her. This was what he had done to so many other unsuspecting young women and girls they'd grabbed off the highways. Forced them to work for him, using their bodies and selling their souls to survive.

She looked around, searching for something…anything that might help her escape. A gun dropped by one of his fallen men, a knife, even a big rock. But there was nothing. She knew Lawson and the others were within hearing distance, knew he was biding his time and making a plan.

She just had to hope that he wouldn't do anything that would end up getting her or both of them hurt in the process.

Chapter Twenty-Four

Lawson growled as he rose to his feet, then strode toward the door the moment he heard Victor Granger's voice. If it hadn't been for Xavier grabbing his arm, he would have been out there before he had realized it.

"Lawson. Hey," Xavier told him. "Stop. Take a breath. Think."

"He's got Sarah," he snarled to Xavier, jerking on his arm to break his hold. But Xavier tightened his grip on Lawson's arm.

Xavier nodded, eyes dark with worry. "I know," he replied. "And I want to get her away from him as much as you do. But you have to keep your head. Victor's relying on you for an emotional reaction so he can take you out. You know that. You have to keep your head, you hear me?"

Lawson yanked his arm free of Xavier's grip, fury racing through his veins. Whether he liked it or not, he knew his friend was right. He couldn't just march out there and confront the man, no matter how much he wanted to. Granger was trying to taunt him into making a mistake. Likely after he had seen the mess they had made of his men.

If anything, this was a good sign, a sign that Granger was a little concerned about what had happened here and what was yet to happen between them. It was hard for Lawson to process any of that right then though. It still felt like Granger had the upper hand since he had Sarah.

He moved to the window, keeping low to get a look at the situation outside. And, sure enough, there they were—Sarah and Granger, outlined against the headlights behind them, his grip on her arm giving her nowhere to go. Her eyes were wide and terrified, a rabbit caught in a snare, and his heart ached seeing her like that. He needed to get her away from him before he and the others could make a move on Granger and what was left of his men.

"We can't get a good shot from up here," Cade muttered through the comm. "The headlights are obscuring him. There's no way we would be able to make sure we wouldn't hit Sarah."

"Hold back then," Xavier replied, seamlessly taking the lead when Lawson needed him to. "Don't take the shot unless you're sure you can take him out without hurting Sarah."

Lawson's mind raced, trying to think of a solution where Sarah could get away from Granger without being hurt. He hated feeling helpless. He could tell from the look in her eyes that she was silently pleading with him to get her out of this in one piece. He had to save her.

The only way Lawson could do that, he decided, was to do what Granger expected him to do, knowing the guys would have his back.

"Xavier, look at me," he ordered him. "I'm going to turn myself over to Granger."

Xavier's eyes narrowed. "Lawson—"

"No. Listen," he said, his voice low as he tucked a gun into the holster at his side. "I can't let anything happen to her. So if that means letting Granger think he has me, I can deal with that. I'm going to surrender on the porch. It's the only way to move this forward."

Xavier frowned but nodded. Lawson could tell his friend didn't exactly like this approach, but it wasn't as though they had any other choice right now. Granger had the upper hand at the moment.

The two of them headed out onto the front porch, the headlights from Victor's vehicle obstructing their view of the man and his goons standing in front of them. If Lawson could just lure Granger away from the lights long enough for Cade or Aaron to take the shot…

And there was Sarah. Granger still held her in front of him, blocking most of his body. Lawson could tell she was trying to be strong, but her pale face and wide eyes gave her away. He wanted nothing more than to rip her out of the man's grasp, pull her into his arms and reassure her everything was going to be okay. He just needed her to hold it together a little longer.

Lawson shifted his gaze back to the man responsible for all of this. Xavier had been right when he told Lawson to keep his wits about him. If he went off half-cocked now, they'd all be dead, and God only knew what terrible fate Sarah would suffer by Granger's hands.

He agreed with his friend's assessment that the man was expecting Lawson to make an emotional decision, and he couldn't let himself fall into that trap. This all would go to hell in a second if he did.

Lawson held his hands out to his sides, showing Granger he wasn't holding a weapon. "I'm here," he told the man.

Granger sneered at him, clearly not buying it. "And what about the rest of your little buddies?" he asked. "Where are they?"

"I sent them away," Lawson lied quickly. "There's no one here but Xavier and me."

Granger took a step toward them with Sarah, the headlights outlining them both as one. Her eyes were pinned to Lawson's, but she didn't acknowledge him or make a sound. That was smart. They only needed one slip from Granger and maybe she could get away and take cover. If Lawson could hold the other man's attention on him, he could give her that chance.

Suddenly, two identical men climbed out of the car behind Granger and Lawson's eyes darted to them. Lyle and Nelson, his sons. They were both armed. Lawson steadied his breathing, hoping Cade and Aaron had clear shots of them from the top floor of the lodge.

"I don't believe you," Granger replied simply. "Lyle, Nelson, clear out the building."

The two men strode forward to do their father's bidding. They had their father's build, and the same dark, hateful eyes. Both carried themselves with a sleek swagger that was powerful and confident. They were overconfident, hopefully. But before they could reach the porch, Granger changed his orders.

"On second thought," he remarked, almost casually, "shoot them both in the head first."

"No!" Sarah screamed and started fighting Granger's hold. Lyle and Nelson rounded on Xavier and Lawson, but before they could lift their weapons, gunfire exploded from the floor above them.

The goons in front of Granger and Sarah scattered, bullets from Cade and Aaron's guns following them as they ran. Nelson cried out a curse as he threw himself toward the porch for cover to avoid the bullets raining down. Xavier was there to intercept him, and grabbed him by the collar of his shirt and slammed him roughly against one of the pillars outside the front door.

The bullets poured down from above, driving Granger

back toward the safety of the car, one arm still wrapped around Sarah, like he knew he wouldn't leave the lodge alive without her in tow. Lawson could hear her fighting him, trying to get free.

"No! Let me go! Lawson!" Her frightful cries pierced his heart. He couldn't go to her yet, though, they still had to take care of the brothers first. They were too much of a threat to them all. Even though Lyle and Nelson were both dodging bullets, they were still armed and it would only take one lucky shot to disable or kill Lawson and Xavier. He prayed she could just hold on a little longer.

Nelson was sliding down the pillar as Xavier landed a kick to his gut, the crack of a rib sounding from the strike. Lyle was a little smarter, trying to raise his gun at Lawson before he darted for cover.

Lawson managed to dive out of the way in the split second before Lyle fired his weapon. Lyle raised his gun to fire again and Lawson jumped up, surprising him. Lawson grabbed Lyle's arm and twisted it up behind his back, forcing him to drop his weapon. Suddenly, Xavier was there pulling Lyle away from Lawson, and forcing him to the ground. Xavier punched him in the face, then slammed his head back into the hard earth a few times until Lyle went limp beneath him.

"Go after Sarah!" he exclaimed. "I've got him!"

Lawson didn't need to be told twice. He turned on his heel and sprinted toward the car, where Granger was dragging Sarah to escape. If he managed to get her off the property, Lawson would likely never see her again. Lawson couldn't let that happen. He had to stop Granger now.

He came in hot, rushing around the back of the car, where he was sure Granger had taken Sarah. But before he could get his bearings, a fist slammed into his stomach, knocking the wind out of him and sending him stumbling backward.

"Lawson!" Sarah screamed, her voice sounding shrill and panicked. He wanted to reassure her that he was okay, but he couldn't speak. He tried to suck in a long breath, but doubled over in pain. For a man as old as he was, Victor Granger knew how to throw a punch.

Before Lawson could stand up fully, Granger was there, knocking him to the ground. His eyes flashed with fury as he pulled back his arm and slammed his fist into Lawson's face over and over. Lawson shoved his arms between them to block the punches and tried to roll to the side to throw him off. Before Lawson could get his legs under him, Granger shoved Lawson onto his back and put his knee on his stomach, the full weight of him pressing down on to his chest as he tried to choke the life out of him.

Lawson tried to get his arms up to grab Granger's hands at his throat, but the man forced them down with his own arms, shifting his grip on Lawson's neck. Even as the darkness started crowding the corners of his vision, Lawson's only thought was of Sarah. And the hope she'd been able to get away.

Chapter Twenty-Five

Sarah stared in horror as Granger attacked Lawson. He never even had a chance to defend himself. That first hit was enough to take his breath and Granger took swift advantage. Now, she stood there frozen, watching as Lawson lay helpless on the ground with Granger hovering over him, choking him to death.

She was terrified, but she had to do something. She couldn't stand there and watch Lawson die and not do anything to try to help. But what? Maybe Xavier would come?

She shifted her gaze to where Xavier had been fighting with the sons. Apparently, Lyle had gotten his second wind. He and Xavier were still throwing punches and from the look in Xavier's eyes, she could tell Lyle didn't stand a chance. She also noticed that Cade was standing off to the side with his weapon pointed at Nelson, who was still groaning on the ground holding his leg. Aaron seemed to be checking Victor's men scattered around the grounds and restraining those still moving.

That left Sarah herself. It was up to her to help Lawson in any way she could.

At first, she leaped on Granger's back, hoping that would surprise him enough to release his hold. The man let out a growl and threw her off to the side. It gave Lawson the opportunity to get his legs free from under Granger and he was using them to kick him wherever he could land blows, hoping to release his grip.

Sarah jumped up and ran to the vehicle beside her, looking around to see if there was something inside it she could use. Quickly scanning the interior, the only things she could see were a half bottle of water and a thin towel on the floor. No. She ripped open the glovebox and shuffled through the contents. Tears filled her eyes. There was absolutely nothing. She angrily swiped at her eyes, clearing her vision, listening to the grunts and groans and gasps filtering in the car from outside.

She chanced another look outside the vehicle and noticed Granger no longer had Lawson pinned to the ground. They were rolling around trading punches, but Granger still seemed to have more of the upper hand, landing more hits than Lawson was able to return. Sarah could see the marks around his neck and knew that had something to do with it. If Lawson was in full fighting form, she knew he'd take the man down with ease.

Her eyes shifted again between the microfiber towel and the water bottle. She couldn't believe these were her only options. Trying not to think about what she was going to do, she grabbed both items and scrambled out of the car.

Granger was back on top of Lawson, holding him down and punching him in the face, the chest, anywhere he could land a blow. Sarah cringed when she heard a crunch and Lawson's painful groan. She clenched the bottle of water in her hand and raced over to them. After uncapping the lid, she threw the water in Granger's face, startling him enough to shift his eyes to her, giving Lawson the opening he needed.

Lawson slammed a fist into the man's side, throwing him

off balance long enough for Lawson to draw a full breath, and then he followed it up with another punch to Granger's nose, a spray of blood leaking down his face. Granger let out a grunt, his head flopping to the right, and she felt a pulse of triumph. Lawson locked his hands together, and then smashed them into Granger's face. The man spat blood, his eyes darkening with a pure malice.

He shoved away Lawson's arms and pressed his own to Lawson's throat again, this time bearing down with all of his weight. He was going to kill him for sure this time. That snapped Sarah out of her daze. She rushed forward again and climbed onto Granger's back, wrapping her arms around his neck and tugging. She kept jerking and jerking with no effect. Granger's rage had completely taken over—he didn't even acknowledge her presence.

Sarah quickly wrapped the towel around his neck, grabbing each end and pulling back with all the force she had. She pushed off his back for leverage and kept tugging on the cloth with all her might. A grunt and gasp were music to her ears. It was working!

She let out her own grunts of frustration and exertion as she tried to pull the man away from Lawson. At last, he lifted his hand and clawed at the cloth around his throat.

Granger stood up, far too easily, and tossed Sarah back toward the car. She slammed into the side, letting out a cry of pain as he rounded on her. She had never seen such unfiltered hatred in someone's eyes before, and she did her best to scramble back and away from him.

Granger dragged a hand across his bloodied nose, smearing scarlet across his face. He looked like a demon, covered in blood, eyes nearly black with fury.

"You're not worth the cash I could make from you," he

told her, spitting a mouthful of blood at the ground next to her.

He moved toward her, a maniacal grin spreading across his face, as though he was going to enjoy exactly what he planned to do next. She scrambled backward, whimpering with fear, trying to kick at him, but her legs felt like jelly. She didn't have any more fight in her.

But a second later, she realized she wasn't going to have to fight. Lawson lunged at him, sending Granger slamming into the side of the car with a sickening crash. He let out a cry of pain, and Sarah tried to crawl away as fast as she could so he couldn't grab her again.

Lawson was on top of him, his eyes wild and his face already starting to bruise. Cuts were scattered across his lip and his brow, dripping blood down his face, but he didn't seem to notice.

Lawson landed punch after punch, slamming his fists without mercy into Granger's head, the forceful hits snapping his neck left and right as he tried to lift his arms to get a blow in. But it was over.

"Stop!" Granger cried out, his mouth bubbling with blood. Lawson was like a machine, delivering jab after jab. He was practiced and skilled enough to render Granger useless. The man tried to lift his arms to cover his head, but Lawson pinned them to the ground beneath his knees, giving him no room to escape.

Her plan worked. She had given him just enough time to react, to recover, and now, he was winning. She watched, unable to speak as she took in the sheer intensity of his brutal assault. And she knew, deep down, that this was for her—this was because Granger had threatened her, threatened them. It was for everyone else, too—the trafficking victims, the lodge, their friends, the future they all wanted. But mostly her.

Police sirens shrieked in the distance, making Sarah jump, as Xavier rounded the corner of the car to grab Lawson's shoulder.

"Hey. Lawson!" he called to him. "It's over, Lawson. Stop. You can stop."

Panting hard, Lawson drew his fist back one last time, and then turned to look up at Xavier. His eyes, which before had seemed so distant, snapped back to reality. Although it was clear he wanted to end Granger right then and there, he had to go to jail. It was the only way his victims were going to be able to get justice for everything he had done.

Lawson rose to his feet, and Xavier flipped over Granger and snapped a pair of cuffs on to his wrists. Lawson's eyes finally found Sarah, and he grinned, a smile so wide it looked as though it could have split his face in two.

"We've got this," Xavier assured him. "Go, your girl needs you."

She really does, Sarah thought as she scrambled off the ground.

Lawson made his way toward her and wrapped his arms around her in an embrace that made the world fall away for a moment. She knew they had been through hell, but right now, all she cared about was feeling safe in his arms, where she belonged.

"Is it over now?" she breathed. She wouldn't be able to believe it until she heard those words come from his lips.

He nodded against her neck. "It's over," he promised her, and he pulled back, looking her up and down. "Are you alright? Did he hurt you?"

"I'm fine," she replied, though she could feel some of the pain from her torn-up hands and bruised back as the adrenaline started to fade from her system. Her body was going to make her pay for this tomorrow, she was sure of it, but right now, she was grateful that she was here with Lawson, that they were both safe.

And most of all, that Victor Granger seemed to have finally been brought to his knees. Hopefully, he would never see the outside of a prison again so he could never hurt another innocent woman.

"You look just as pretty as your sons right now," Xavier taunted Granger as he stood over him. The man's head turned to the side so he could see both his sons bloodied and bruised, sitting cuffed on the ground with Cade and Aaron standing guard over them and Granger's few men who had survived the attack.

He knew it was over and he was going to pay for everything he had done.

"Hope nobody you're in prison with finds out what you're in for," Xavier continued, a grin spreading across his face. "They don't take too kindly to sex traffickers."

Sarah sank into Lawson's arms again, closing her eyes and focusing on the feel of his chest rising and falling against her ear. She was sure what came next was going to be chaos, but she didn't care. She was where she belonged right now.

And nothing in the world could take that away from her.

Chapter Twenty-Six

The moon was high in the sky above as the front of the lodge was suddenly lit up with multiple glowing lights. Several cop cars screeched to a halt around them, swiftly followed by the paramedics. Lawson held Sarah close, trying to block out all of the noise and activity around them and just concentrate on how she felt in his arms.

He could feel her tears against his shirt, and he hated that she was so upset right now, but he reminded himself that things could be so much worse.

"I'm so sorry," he murmured to her, brushing his lips over the top of her head. "I thought I was protecting you by sending you away from the lodge but I should have known that the safest place for you to be is by my side."

"It's okay," she replied, lifting her gaze to meet his. "I know you were just trying to do the right thing. I don't blame you."

He smiled at her, and leaned down to plant a kiss against her lips as the sheriff hopped out of his car behind them.

"Sorry it took us so long to get here, but it looks like you guys have it handled. Granger had a few surprises set up for us along the way and the FBI is dealing with that. SWAT is currently securing the outer area," Sheriff Willis volunteered, as Lawson pulled back from Sarah. "So what's the status here? Who do I need to cuff?" he demanded.

"We're just glad you made it, Sheriff. Xavier has them," Lawson replied, directing him to the other man, who was still standing over Granger. "He'll tell you what you need to know."

"Good," Sheriff Willis replied, nodding sharply and walking toward the two men. "This way, men! Let's round them up," the sheriff added, directing his deputies to Granger's men scattered around the ground.

Just then, Bailey's car pulled up behind the sheriff's vehicle. All three women sprang out and rushed to Sarah's side

"Are you oka—" Hannah began.

"What happened?" Bailey asked, speaking over her.

"Where are—" River began at the same time, but Sarah just pointed them back toward the lodge.

"Over there," she replied. "They're waiting for you."

River and Bailey ran off toward the lodge, while Hannah rushed to where Xavier was standing, talking with the sheriff. She practically leaped into Xavier's arms when she reached him. Lawson couldn't help but smile, glad that they had all found each other again. He still felt guilty for sending Sarah away in the first place, but that line of thought would have to wait. There was so much more they had to take care of before he could replay everything that had happened.

Once Hannah had extracted herself from Xavier's arms, she took his hand and came over to talk to Lawson and Sarah.

"Are you okay?" she asked her brother, fussing over him as she took in the bruises and cuts on his face. He knew he would be looking rough come the morning, but right now, he could hardly feel it. He was sure the paramedics would want to give him a once-over to make sure he was okay, but the important thing was Lawson had survived. Hurt like hell, but he would make it.

"Yeah, I'm fine," he replied.

"And you, Sarah?" she asked with concern. "Oh, God, I was so scared when you got out of the car like that."

"You did *what*?" Lawson asked, confused. He thought Granger had intercepted the women and forced Sarah to give herself up to him.

"I knew they wanted me," she said softly, shrugging. "I thought it would give the others a chance to get away if I pretended to turn myself over to them, but I had to run instead."

He stared down at her. He could hardly believe it. He squeezed her closer, hating the thought of her sacrificing herself like that, but even more in awe of her than he had been before, which he hadn't thought was possible.

"I thought we might never see you again," Hannah blurted, her voice wracked with emotion. Lawson tensed. There it was, the horror that he had almost faced.

He had almost lost her. And the thought of it made him feel sick. It was worse than any of the physical pain he had endured that night, by a long shot. He closed his eyes and pressed his face into her hair, reminding himself that she was safe. That was what he needed to remember, above all else, and he was never going to let any threat get that close to her again.

But there was someone else out there who needed his help right now. Lainey was still out there somewhere. Granger wanted him to think that she was dead, but there was no way Lawson would give up until he knew for sure.

"Are you going to be okay?" he asked her.

"Yeah, I'll be fine," she murmured. "What about you?"

"There's something else I need to do," he told her. "I'll meet you at the hospital, alright?"

"Don't get hurt," she pleaded with him, and he kissed her cheek.

"I promise I won't," he replied. "But there's someone else I need to get back to their family in one piece."

She squeezed his hand, and then one of the paramedics led her away so she could get checked over. He watched as she went, feeling a pang at the thought of leaving her again, but he promised himself it wasn't going to be for long. Soon enough, he would be back by her side.

He stalked over to Granger, who was being held along with both of his sons inside a cop car. All of them were cuffed and looked worse for wear, though what they had waiting in front of them was far worse than anything Xavier or Lawson could have inflicted on them with their fists and weapons.

Lawson yanked open the door, startling the men inside. "Where's Lainey?" he demanded, reaching inside the car, grabbing Granger by the collar.

The man grinned at him, teeth smeared with blood. "You really think I'm going to tell you where that bitch is?" he asked. "Let her rot. If we're going to prison, she can stay in hers, too."

Lawson grimaced. Okay, so he wasn't going to get the information out of Granger, but maybe his sons would be quicker to crack. He looked at them.

"Lyle, Nelson," he snapped. "You want a couple of years cut off your sentence?"

"Yes," Lyle blurted out. His face was pale where it wasn't marked with blood or bruises. They were looking down the barrel of a long life in prison for helping their father with his crimes, and he figured they would want to do anything they could to try to shorten their time behind bars.

Though Lawson knew damn well he couldn't cut them

a deal like that, he was willing to try anything he could to get them to hand over Lainey's location.

"Then you tell me where she's being held," he continued, lowering his voice so it didn't travel beyond the back seat and the three men inside. He didn't want them trying to use what he had said to wheedle their way out of the sentence they deserved, and he was going to use everything he had at his disposal to get them to talk.

"Don't say a damn word," Granger warned his sons.

Lawson watched the two brothers closely. Indecision flickered across both their faces before their eyes darted to their father's. Lawson's pulse jumped in anticipation. One of them was about to crack, he could tell. Granger could tell too, if his face turning a concerning shade of red was any indication. Looked like whatever power the man once had over his sons was gone.

"There's a compound, just outside of town," Lyle said quickly, like he wanted to be the one to tell him. "And I… She's being held in a back room there. The code for the building's main door lock is two-six-three-one."

"Address," Lawson ordered. "Now."

"It's where the old dairy farm used to be," Nelson revealed. "It always stunk of old milk."

Granger growled, trying to tell them not to say anything else, but that was all Lawson needed to hear from them. He slammed the car door shut and headed over to Sheriff Willis.

"You know where the old dairy farm outside of town is?" he demanded.

"Yeah, about an hour from here," the sheriff replied. "Why? You got a craving for cheese all of a sudden?"

Lawson managed to let out a laugh, despite the circumstances. He shook his head. "They're holding my friend Lainey there," he replied. "I need to get to her."

"I'll take you there myself," the sheriff replied. "My officers have this under control. They're taking this personally, after what happened at the station."

Lawson nodded in understanding. He knew the horror of what had gone down that day would live long in the memory of the town. Blue Ridge had never had any incidents of that magnitude.

Sheriff Willis and Lawson climbed into the sheriff's car and sped away from the lodge. Time was of the essence since they didn't know how long Lainey had been held or what condition she was in. The sheriff radioed in what was happening and a few other vehicles joined them on the road. Lawson looked over his shoulder to see who all was following them.

"Who's with us?" Lawson asked warily.

"A SWAT unit and the FBI," the sheriff replied. "When the women came racing into town for help, they busted in the station while I was finishing up with the FBI. They filled us in on what they knew, that Granger and his men would be attacking the lodge soon and about Sarah. We had already devised a plan and were about to split up to put it in motion. I tried to reach you guys, but they must have already taken out the communications."

Lawson grimaced. They could have used them earlier at the lodge, but at least they were helping with the cleanup now, and to get Lainey. Might not be a bad thing to have them along in case Granger had any more men hanging around their base of operation. Lawson hadn't thought to ask the man's sons. He was just concentrating on getting to his friend as fast as possible. He had no idea how long they'd actually had her or what had been done to her.

One thing he did know, though, was now her superiors had to take the information she'd given them and do something about it. Pass everything along through the proper channels to see that Victor Granger and his sons got the punishment they deserved. And Lainey would be free to return to her family.

They just needed to find her alive. Lawson knew she was a fighter, since that's what had gotten her into this mess in the first place. Not being able to let something go or someone else take the reins. He just had to hope she'd kept a level head through it all so Granger hadn't felt the need to get rid of her.

Eventually, the sheriff pulled the car to a halt outside a run-down factory; there were several fresh tire marks outside, a sure sign that it had been used recently. Lawson climbed out of the car cautiously, eyes darting around to make sure there were no men left over to guard the place, but it looked like all of them had been sent to the attack on the lodge.

The SWAT team and FBI vehicles pulled up behind them. Agents fanned out to search the grounds and the building. Before Lawson could offer them the code Lyle had given him, they blasted the door. Lawson rushed in behind them, glancing around, calling out for Lainey. For a moment, a dark, unsettling silence hung over the place.

As the group he was with moved farther into the building, they heard more gunshots echoing around. Apparently, there were some men left there after all. A voice sounded over their comm unit, relaying that everything was clear, and the team Lawson was with proceeded.

Nothing but an eerie quiet greeted them the deeper they went. Then suddenly, he heard it. A pounding noise and a muffled voice called through the door at the end of the corridor.

Relief flooded him all at once. It had to be Lainey.

"I heard something. Check down there," he told the SWAT leader standing beside him, and the men raced forward and busted the door down.

Sure enough, there was Lainey.

"Oh, thank God," he muttered as he pushed through the small crowd to reach her. She was chained up to a chair, her head lolling down to her chest, her face riddled with bruises and cuts.

She lifted her head up when she heard Lawson's voice, and a couple of the team set about trying to free her from her chains. Her dull eyes lit up and she tried to grin, though it turned into a grimace. Lawson could tell she was in a lot of pain.

"You found me," she muttered through her swollen lips, her voice weak. Looked like they might have broken her jaw. Her face was so swollen and bruised, her eyes looked like a couple of seeds in a watermelon.

"I would never leave you behind, Lainey," he promised her. "Come on, let's get you out of here and checked out. Then we can get you back to your family."

Still sitting, she fell forward into Lawson as soon as she was free. She was beaten up pretty badly and was holding her side, but she was alive. That was what mattered.

"Victor Granger's done?" she asked him.

"He's done," he promised her. "You're never going to have to deal with him again, except to testify against him in court and put him behind bars for the rest of his life."

She squeezed her eyes shut, and a tear leaked down her face. With Lawson's help, she got to her feet and gave him as much of a hug as she could, groaning through the pain it caused her.

"Thank you," she breathed. "I wouldn't have been able to do this without you, Lawson."

"You're welcome," he replied sincerely as he put an arm around her and helped her limp toward the door. After being tied up for so long, he was sure her legs were starting to ache just from moving again.

He raised an eyebrow at her. "Just promise you haven't got any more cases you're going to drag me into, yeah?"

She tried to laughed. "I promise. After this, I think I'm done for life. I don't want to look at another case again."

"Let's get you to the hospital," he told her.

"Yes, please. Some type of pain meds sounds really good right about now," she replied.

He chuckled and shook his head. "I'm sure the doctors can hook you up with some good stuff," he replied firmly.

"I don't want to put you out—these guys can take me," she offered.

Lawson shook his head. "I think I'll make sure you get there in one piece." Besides, he needed to go there, anyway. He had his own injuries to get looked at.

And because that was where he'd find Sarah. He wanted to hold her, and tell her that, at last, it was all over.

Chapter Twenty-Seven

Sarah paced back and forth in the waiting room as she counted out the minutes since Lawson had arrived. She wasn't sure exactly how much longer it was going to take him to get patched up, but she felt as though she was going crazy while she waited.

He had arrived at the hospital nearly two hours ago with a woman she assumed was Lainey. They'd both been surrounded by medical personnel and taken back to the treatment area as soon as the staff got a look at them.

Sarah had already been looked at and patched up. Her hands had been tended to and disinfected, but she couldn't go anywhere until she knew that Lawson was okay. She kept watching the doors they'd disappeared behind, willing Lawson to walk out.

"I'm sure he's fine," Hannah tried to reassure her. She was sitting on one of the hard plastic chairs that lined the wall, leaning into Xavier's side.

"Yeah, I'm sure most of his injuries are superficial," Xavier agreed. "You know he'd want you to go back to the lodge and get some rest."

She shook her head. "I can't go yet," she replied firmly. "I need to know he's okay."

"Who's okay?" a rough voice behind her asked.

Sarah's head snapped around when she heard Lawson's voice. She breathed a long sigh of relief when she saw him standing there and went over to wrap her arms around him.

"Oh, my God." She sighed, leaning against his chest. "You're okay?"

"Pretty much," he replied, but she could hear the wince in his voice.

She sprang back from him at once. "Oh, sorry, I didn't even think," she blurted out, scanning him for injuries. "What's the damage?"

He reached out a hand to Sarah and drew her back to his side. "A couple of cracked ribs," he responded. "Throat contusion, some cuts and bruises, and a broken finger."

He lifted his hand, to show the splint on his finger. His face had been cleaned up and patched, and it looked a lot better now that it wasn't smeared in blood.

"Really. That's all?" she asked. She had been so scared he'd end up with serious damage after his fight with Granger. She was so relieved all his injuries seemed mostly minor. His neck, though… She shuddered at the swift memory of Granger with his hands wrapped around Lawson's throat.

"Hey, that's nothing to sniff at." He tried to laugh, wincing again, and raised his injured hand to his neck.

"I'm sorry. I mean, I'm just glad it's not worse," she replied, taking his good hand and giving it a squeeze. "What happens now?"

Lawson and Xavier exchanged a look. "Well, I gave my statement to the FBI while I was being fixed up. They're still back there talking to Lainey. They'll be contacting the rest of you to get statements in the next few days. I told them they'd find us all at the lodge."

"How's Lainey," Xavier asked. "Did she mention how she ended up at the old dairy farm?"

"Apparently, Donner grabbed her after he escaped and was leaving town. Just dumb luck he ran into her and recognized her from a photo Granger had been passing around. She'll need some time to heal, but she'll be fine," Lawson replied with a smile. "Once she's released, the FBI will see she gets back home to her family."

"Speaking of family," Xavier interjected. "We should get back to the lodge and see the damage. There's a lot that needs to be done."

"Yeah, the others are back already," Hannah added, rising to her feet. Xavier draped an arm around her protectively.

"There's going to be a lot in the way of repairs and cleanup. Again." Lawson sighed.

"You need to rest," Sarah protested, but he just smiled at her.

"I'm okay," he replied. "I want to know what we're going to be dealing with. Then I'll be able to relax."

"The sheriff has a couple of his guys ready to run us back to the lodge," Xavier explained. "Come on, let's get out of here."

ON THE WAY back to the lodge, the sun had begun to rise. Sarah sat plastered to Lawson's side in the back of the police car, not leaving any room between them. Not that either of them minded. He wrapped his arm around her and pulled her closer.

It was a new start, a new opportunity for them to turn the lodge into the safe space it was always meant to be. With Victor Granger gone, it felt like the way was finally clear for Sarah and Lawson to be together, like they had wanted to be for so long.

Arriving back on the property, Sarah was surprised to see

that there were already a few cars scattered around, parked in the driveway. She frowned, worried.

"What's all this?" she muttered as they climbed out of the car. Bailey waved to her from the porch, grinning as a few people walked past her into the building.

"What's going on here?" Lawson asked, sounding confused.

"When we got back from the hospital we noticed the bodies had been removed, and the FBI were packing up their evidence, ready to leave," Aaron replied. "Told us we could start cleanup whenever we were ready."

"And apparently, while the guests were in town, word got around that the lodge had been attacked," Cade called back to Lawson as he emerged from inside. "After the FBI cleared out, people started showing up with supplies. Seems like we have a lot more friends than we thought."

Sarah's lips parted with surprise. "They came to help?" she asked.

"Excuse me!" someone called behind her, and she turned to see a man heading toward them with a large pane of glass under one arm. She stepped aside for him to walk past her, staring after him until he disappeared through the entrance.

"Yeah, Sheriff Willis also called in some help from the officers," Bailey told them as she headed down from the porch. "And a few other people from town also wanted to give us a hand, when they found out what happened and that we'd helped stop the criminal organization that had been terrorizing the roads around here. This place is going to be back on its feet in no time."

"That's amazing news," Sarah replied, a rush of emotion rising through her chest. This was so kind of people who were basically strangers to come up and help put the place back in order. It was such a great feeling, knowing people cared enough to help get the lodge back up and running again.

"You want some coffee?" River asked as she popped her head through the front door. "I just got a pot on. I figured it's going to be too noisy to get any sleep, at least anytime soon."

"Sounds good to me," Hannah replied, tugging on Xavier's hand to lead him inside. Sarah followed behind them, and smiled when she saw the industrious hard work taking place around her. It was seriously incredible; she could hardly believe what she was seeing.

Several hours ago, this place had been a complete disaster. And although it still had a long way to go, it already looked better.

They all walked through to the kitchen, where River and Cade were passing out coffees. Sarah wrapped her hands around hers gratefully, inhaling the scent. She was tired, sure, but too full of excitement to go to bed yet. And the feel of Lawson's strong arm around her shoulders was enough to ground her and give her all the peace she needed. Bailey and Aaron laughed about something at the far end of the counter, both of them practically giddy with relief.

"Where do we even start?" Xavier asked.

Cade shook his head. "I think they're determined to take care of everything for us," he replied, gesturing around them. "I mean, we'll probably still be picking bullet fragments out of the main building for the next year..."

"But the hardest part is already dealt with," River insisted. She looked so relaxed, and it made Sarah so happy to see her unwinding after the stressful few weeks they'd had. Stressful months, if she was being honest.

"Yeah, and then we'll have to think about putting Victor Granger and his sons behind bars," Bailey added as she joined the group.

"We can handle that when we have to. The FBI has it under control," Aaron replied, shaking his head. "For now, I think we deserve to celebrate. Right?"

"Well, I don't know if coffee has quite the same ring to it that champagne does." Hannah giggled. "But how about a toast? To the lodge?"

"To the lodge," Lawson agreed, and he lifted his mug. Around him, everyone repeated the sentiment, tapping their mugs against the others and then taking a long sip.

Afterward, the couples drifted off to see where they could help out, and Sarah finished up her coffee and sighed.

"I guess I should find some way to make myself useful, huh?" she remarked, smiling up at Lawson.

He gazed down at her for a moment, and then pressed a kiss against her forehead. "I'm so proud of the way you handled yourself last night," he murmured to her.

"What do you mean?" she asked, slightly confused. She had succeeded in getting herself kidnapped by Granger. She didn't see how that was anything to be proud of.

"I mean, you were willing to sacrifice yourself to keep the rest of the women safe," he replied. "Not many people would have the nerve to do that. You're the bravest woman I know."

She leaned into him for a moment, and then he cocked his head at her with a playful smile on his face.

"By the way," he remarked. "Was that a towel you attacked Granger with?"

She let out a slightly shaky laugh. "It might have been."

He laughed. "You're crazy, woman," he replied. "And I love you."

Those words hung there between them. For a second, Sarah froze. There's no way he just said what she thought he did, right? She locked her gaze with his.

"You…?" She couldn't get any other words out.

"I love you," he repeated, not wavering for a second as he gazed at her. "I love you for your strength, your bravery and your kindness. How you keep surprising me. And because you were willing to wait for me, even though I took my damn time getting my head out of my ass. I love you, Sarah."

She giggled, the sound light and magical to his ears, and cupped her hand gently around his cheek.

She leaned in slowly to plant a kiss on his lips, not breaking eye contact. "I love you, too, Lawson," she replied.

Before she could say another word, he moved into her and deepened the kiss.

All at once, the chaos surrounding them seemed to fall away, leaving nothing but the two of them, in their embrace.

She wanted to stay there forever.

Epilogue

"Here, let me help," Lawson told Sarah, offering her a hand to climb down on to the rocks next to the clear blue natural pool below the waterfall. She picked her way down toward the water in her sneakers, the sun gleaming off her legs beneath her shorts. He tried not to let his gaze linger on the sight of her like that, but damn, it was hard not to feel like a teenager around her.

"Made it!" she told him happily, as she sank down on to the edge of the rocks, kicked off her shoes and dipped her feet in the water. "Mmm, that feels so good."

He grinned as he sat down next to her, taking out the contents of the bag they packed full of food and fresh lemonade from the kitchen.

When he'd woken early on that Sunday morning and saw the late summer sun pouring through the window, he'd known he wanted to finally take her up to his favorite spot, just the two of them.

Now, here they were, by the pool at the bottom of a waterfall that stood high in the mountains above the lodge. It was a bit of a hike to get there, but the peace and quiet was exactly what he wanted for her.

"This is exactly what I needed." She sighed, closing her eyes and leaning back on her elbows as the sun bathed her face. He looked down at her for a moment. It was these instances, just the two of them in the quiet, where he realized how much he loved her. How safe and settled he felt when she was around.

Of course, they'd known each other for several years, but it was only now that he was able to be truly and totally honest with himself about his feelings for her.

"Good," he murmured, pushing a glass of lemonade into her hand. "Here you go. I think we could both use a drink after that hike."

"Thanks," she replied, smiling at him as she took a sip of the tart, sweet lemonade Hannah had made earlier that week.

"So how's therapy going?" he asked her.

She paused for a moment, considering the question, and then replied, "Overall, it's been good, I think. Not easy by any means, especially since we moved it up to three times a week. But I want to make sure I have my head straight for Granger's trial."

"But you're coping with everything okay?" he asked. "It must be intense, working through all that happened."

"It is," she admitted. "But it's not impossible. And besides, it's not going to be forever. The trial's finally in a couple of months, and I can step back some after that. Refocus on other things and move past all this once and for all."

"Good point," he agreed. "You're doing great, Sarah. You should be really proud of yourself."

"I'm a therapist—of course, I'm good at therapy," she joked.

Suddenly, she jumped up, pulled off her shirt and wiggled out of her shorts. She flashed Lawson a flirty grin, slipping into the water below. "Come join me, it's so nice in here..." she said, flipping to float on her back.

He didn't need to be told twice. He quickly stripped

off his own clothes and dove into the water alongside her. He used to come to this spot all the time last summer, to think through problems and reflect on what all they'd been through and where he'd like to see them going. But there was something about sharing it with her that was a million times more special.

He used to think that he wouldn't be able to let anyone get close to him. He was scared to be vulnerable with someone and to let them see the real him, underneath the tough-guy exterior. But he had never once doubted that letting Sarah into his life was the right call. He just hated that he'd waited for so long to make it happen.

He was just grateful that Sarah was patient and that she loved him, despite his tendency to be hardheaded. He intended to keep her in his life forever.

She swam toward him, resting her arms on his shoulders and smiling at him. He pushed her hair back from her face, gazing into her eyes. Sometimes he still couldn't believe that after all this time, she was his.

"What about you?" she asked, brushing her nose against his.

"What about me?" he replied.

"What are you going to do after the trial?" she said.

"What do you mean?" he asked, confused. He would have to testify, too, of course, but he didn't expect it to be that big of a deal for him. He'd dealt with plenty of people like Victor Granger over the years, and standing up against them in court wasn't new to him. In fact, he was eager to tell the truth about Granger and to get him locked up for good.

"I mean…" she began, trailing off for a moment, like she wasn't quite sure how to put it. "Do you have any other missions you might take on? Anything else that Lainey has asked you to do?"

He shook his head. Lainey was back home and settled with her family again and she was doing well. She'd invited him and Sarah down for a visit at the end of the year, around the holidays, and they had already made a pact not to talk business.

"Nothing that I know of," he replied. "Why do you ask?"

"Just…curious, that's all," she replied coyly, a little smile on her face. "I want to know where you see your life in a year. Or two years. Or ten."

"And why might that be?" he asked her, though he already knew the answer. Though the two of them hadn't actually discussed what was coming next for them, their love for each other was obvious. If he could spend the rest of his life waking up next to her, he would, and he hoped she knew that.

They had moved into one of the resident cabins together down by the others, and his sister and the other women were thrilled at having Sarah closer for them to hang out and gossip with. They decided to leave her separate cabin empty and usable for any of their residents who might need more intensive therapy, or couldn't handle being in closer quarters with others.

Lawson loved being able to see her first thing in the morning and last thing at night before he closed his eyes. To spend more quality time together just enjoying each other's company, or sipping on coffee every morning before they went about their daily tasks at the lodge—which had been completely fixed up and repaired by the folks who had shown up in the aftermath on that fateful day last year. Now, thanks to all their help, the lodge was better than when they first started out and thriving more than it ever had before.

He and Xavier finally had their dream come true for Warrior Peak Sanctury. It was truly now a safe place for people to come to for help and treatment and to find themselves again. No danger or destruction or old ghosts reappearing. It was a place of calm and reflection and caring and safety.

"Because I want a real life with you," she confessed. "A family. I want to be a mom one day. I want us to raise kids together, Lawson. But that's going to mean a safe life. You know? Not one where you're running off on tactical missions all the time."

"Hmm. I like the sound of that," he murmured, sealing his mouth over hers once more.

"You mean that?" she asked softly as she pulled back, brushing her nose against his. "It's not going to get too boring for you?"

"Are you kidding?" He chuckled. "Having a life with you? That sounds like the most exciting mission in the world to me."

She giggled, and gazed up at him. "Well, that's a hell of a lot to live up to," she pointed out.

"Yeah?" he replied, slipping his arms around her waist and pulling her as close as possible, so there was no space between their bodies.

"I think you can handle it." He kissed her again, smiling into the embrace. She let out a long breath against his mouth, as though this was what she had been waiting to hear all this time. He would make it clear to her every way he could, every time she asked.

"I love you, Sarah," he told her softly.

"I love you, too," she whispered back, and she kissed him again, the taste of lemonade on her lips. He might have waited too long to make her his, but now, she belonged to him and he belonged to her. He knew he was going to spend the rest of his life making up for lost time, and he was looking forward to every moment.

They had all the time in the world to enjoy together now.

To enjoy building a life and a family with one another, and he could hardly wait to get started.

With the love of his life in his arms, everything felt possible.

* * * * *